PAMELA CUNNINGHAM

Do you Believe in Shooting Stars?

Copyright

In memory of my parents Herbie and Janet Cunningham with my love and thanks. My father for his talent in regaling a good tale and my mother for her talent in spinning one.

Their love for each other, and their absolute conviction that they would be reunited in the afterlife, is the inspiration for this book.

Prologue

Between Celestial dimensions

Myles knows he's travelled the length of this tunnel before, only now he's walking away from the comforting light and into dense swirling fog. He has no idea how long he's been navigating this cloying moisture. Time is irrelevant in this place. He feels afraid. A sensation alien to him. The rumble of thunder reaches him. He feels the vibration, senses the gathering energy, and hope soars. He waits, but still there is nothing more than interminable fog.

Then he sees them, tiny specks of light darting like fireflies piercing the gloom, and he knows the planets have shifted. It has begun. A myriad of voices clamouring to be heard engulfs him. The effort to decipher the individual is draining his energy. With a final supreme effort, he channels the last of his reserve and suddenly he hears the voice he's been waiting for, pure and soothing, nurturing life into his soul. She is the one chosen to be his guide on earth. She will not remember him. Not recognise the face she has once loved so dearly. Her life on earth has begun

1

anew and must be lived again. No, she will not know him, but he will know her, for she is his soul mate and his heart is already aching with longing. The light when it comes is swift and blinding, encapsulating him in a spinning golden sphere travelling at light speed through to earth's dimension.

Chapter One

Midsummer's Eve 2016

Lydia turned over her pillow, punched it once and sank gratefully into the cool fabric. The night was hot and airless and although the rumble of thunder had kept her awake, the promised rain hadn't come. She gave up on her struggle for sleep and rubbing her gritty eyes she staggered into the bathroom to get a drink of water. Damp tendrils clung to her face and she brushed them away cursing the humidity for frizzing her natural curls into something resembling a dandelion clock.

She opened the bathroom window and breathed in the slightly cooler air. The sky was aglow with stars. As she watched, one star shone brighter than the rest, its trail emblazoned across the sky.

'Find me my perfect English gentleman,' she whispered. 'Make him gallant and kind. Let him whisk me away to some other time and place, away from the madness of modern-day life.' She shivered despite the heat, and as the last speck of starlight flared and vanished behind gathering clouds, she shut the window and locked it. Wide awake now, she decided to go downstairs to her shop to get her sketch pad. It wouldn't be the first time she'd been struck by inspiration in the wee small hours. She didn't bother switching on the lights, the moon was bright enough to light the way. It shone in through the shop window sending a shaft of silvery blue light to puddle in the centre of the floor. Enchanted, she stepped into the spotlight. Surprised by the moon's warmth she lifted her face and standing on tiptoe opened her arms as though preparing for flight. 'Calling down the moon,' she whispered, reciting the ancient love charm she remembered from somewhere. Spells and potions may have lost their way in the modern world, but just for tonight, in this most magical of moments, she yearned for those long ago romantic days of pure love. Slowly, she began to sway, twirling and dancing bathed in the moon's light, weaving the magic into her fantasy accompanied by illusive shadows flickering and jumping in step to her rhythm.

The shadows, no longer comforting, danced on to their own tune. She stood transfixed, watching them leaping and cavorting just beyond reach of the moonlight. Blinking, she shook her head trying to clear the images. When her eyes focused again, the shadows had gone but the air was so charged with electricity she could almost hear it crackling. The moon slipped behind the clouds plunging the room into darkness. She stood still, listening. All was quiet, waiting. Moonlight flooded the room, spurring her into action. In two strides, she'd crossed the room and flicked on the light switch. Pain shot up her arm as blue flames arced across her wrist, the explosion above sent glass raining down, the shards pierced her arms as she tried to protect her head.

In the quiet aftermath, she crouched in the darkness surrounded by broken glass. Her right arm tingled and she could feel blood trickling. Gradually, her eyes adjusted to the dark and she scanned the room. Everything seemed as it should be, no lingering shadows. The static energy had evaporated. Then all at once the air was filled with the scent of honeysuckle, the sweet spicy fragrance brought with it a feeling of contentment, as though evoking some long-forgotten memory. She looked around trying to locate its source, her focus was drawn to the hat display by the window. She studied it for some time before she realised what was different. It was perfectly intact, yet somehow, all the hats had switched places.

Chapter Two

Grant Stevenson stood at his New York office window and watched the electrical storm crisscross a sky streaked scarlet by a departing sun. It made a dramatic backdrop for Manhattan's silhouette. The city that never sleeps had been plunged into darkness by nature's force. Silver whips lashed out at the tallest towers and thunder claps shook the building.

'Grant, are you still here?' an anxious voice whispered into the darkness.

'Belle? is that you? I'm over here by the window.' Lightning flashed, illuminating her white face peering at him from the doorway.

She used the moment of brightness to dash across the room just as a bolt of lightning struck a building nearby. 'It's not just the storm,' she said, 'I thought I was all alone up here. The elevator's out and so are the phones. I couldn't even get a signal on my cell phone. I'm so glad you're here, everyone else seems to have gone.'

He could feel her trembling. 'What are you doing working this late on Friday night?'

'I'm supposed to be meeting a friend. Her shift at the hospital finishes around nine-thirty so I thought I'd catch up on some paper work and then get ready here. It saves trailing across town and back again. Do you usually work this late at the weekend?'

'Often! And usually much later than this. But tonight, I was just about to leave. I'm supposed to be flying down to the ranch. I've been going there whenever I can. There's been a lot to sort through since Gramps died. Now it looks like I'll be going nowhere anytime soon.'

'Oh, the lights are back on. No signal on my cell phone yet though. Let's check the elevator.' They walked along a corridor eerily quiet except for the click of her heels. 'We're out of luck, power's still off.'

'It looks like it's only the emergency lighting that's kicked in. The elevators work off a separate generator. We'll be here for a while yet, unless you want to walk down hundreds of stairs.' He turned his head to look out of the window. Rain splattered against the glass and ran down in silvery beads. 'It's raining cats and dogs out there.' he said, 'You'll get soaked.'

'Cats and dogs?'

'It's an English expression. My folks originate from there, it's a family tradition that the children have an English nanny. It was one of her favourite sayings, along with the rain's coming down in stair rods.'

'I can see why they say the eccentric English,' she laughed. 'Gosh I'm starving; I haven't eaten since lunch.'

'Me neither, come on let's see what we can find in the crash pad.' He pushed against a section of cedar wood panelling lining one wall. It sprang open and she followed him into an entirely different world from his high tech minimalist office. He saw her face turn from curious to delight as she took in the battered leather Chesterfield sofa and matching high back winged armchair.

She walked across to the leather top walnut desk and ran a hand along the smooth, well used green leather. 'Nice Art Deco piece you got here.'

'A hand me down from my great-grandfather, Gramps' dad. Try the chair, it spins.'

She sat on the leather seat and gripped the polished arms. The wooden frame topping the spindles, formed both back and arm rest in one semi-circle. 'It's like the newspaper boss's chair in the old black and white movies.'

'Got it in one,' he said, and reached over to spin her around. She tucked her feet up and threw back her head laughing. Her shiny brown hair dangled almost to the floor.

'Enough already, do you want to make me sick?' She grabbed his hand and laughing they went into the kitchen in search of food.

They raided the refrigerator and found a rather grand feast: French bread, Brie, cold chicken, caviar and ice-cream and a very expensive bottle of Champagne. They ate their picnic on the rug – a Native American weave – in front of an authentic looking driftwood fire. He and Belinda, or Belle as she preferred, had dated from time to time, but he had never let her into his inner sanctum, this place which expressed his essence better than anything.

'Cheers,' he said, lifting his glass aloft. 'Here's hoping for a speedy return to the twenty-first century. Actually, I'd better start looking for some candles; I don't know how long the generator will last.'

He came back carrying a tray of tea lights and set it down on the desk. 'You know, I can drive you home, if you want to tackle the stairs.'

'Do you want me to leave? Maybe you could pick up a late flight.'

'I think that the flights will have been affected too, so no I'm happy to sit tight. It wasn't desperate that I go this weekend. It's been a while since the funeral and my parents are mostly on top of things. I guess I just like being there whenever I can. As much as I miss Gramps, I'm ashamed to say I've been using his death as an excuse to go down to the ranch. The lifestyle suits me better than New York.'

'Couldn't you operate the business from there just as easily?' she said, and he sensed a slight edge to her voice.

'I suppose I could, but the hub has always been New York. I'll move to the ranch permanently someday, maybe sooner if I have kids.' He saw a flicker of hope in her eyes and it triggered warning bells in him. Although he'd taken her to dinner a time or two he wasn't in love with her. He didn't want to hurt her and he'd tried to distance himself hoping she'd realise that what they had was casual. But his relentless work schedule left him little time to socialise and on lonely nights it was all too easy to fall into her welcoming arms.

'Hey,' he said, trying to lighten the mood. 'Look what we found in Gramps' attic,' and he reached for two frames propped up against the wall. He set them down side by side on the desk.

'Is that you?'

'No, we think it's my great-grandfather, Gramps' dad, I've seen some photographs of him. He still looked like that as an old man, except his hair was white. My dad can just about remember him. He died when dad was very young.'

'He sure looks like you. It's the blonde hair, almost the same cut and he has the same devilish blue eyes.'

'Devilish?'

'Mischievous then. Look at them they're twinkling right out of the portrait. Who's the woman?'

'We presume she's my great-grandmother. The brass plaques are badly corroded; I'm going to see if they can be restored. Then we might discover who they are for sure.'

'I wonder if her eyes really were that colour violet.' Belle said, 'Her hair is as dark, as his is fair, it's like black silk.'

He moved the portraits to one side and replaced them with a wallet of legal looking documents bound in green ribbon. 'These are the deeds for some place called Barringham Hall and this is a blue print for a refurbishment. These here are the interior designs. We found them tucked away in a cupboard under the eaves in the same box as the portraits.'

'They're early Art Deco,' Belle said, studying the colourful sketches, 'will you use them in one of the hotels?'

'Maybe, when the time's right. Just now folks want minimalist clean lines and that's fine by me, it's quick and cheap.' He was getting bored with the small talk. He was too tired. He picked up his drink and settled back against the sofa. She joined him on the floor, her head propped against his shoulder. He felt content for a while to sit and gaze into the flames.

'Time for a refill,' he said, lifting the bottle. She handed over her empty glass and the tips of her hair trailed the length of his arm. A ripple of desire stirred. He chose to ignore it. Instead, he leisurely sipped the fizzing Champagne and watched the light in her emerald eyes smoulder. Just as leisurely she set down her glass and then taking his, she leaned forward to trace his lips with the tip of her tongue. He crushed her to him and the heat of her breasts burned into his skin. All thoughts of chivalry fled from his mind as they rolled together onto the rug.

Grant slipped silently from his bed and studied Belle in sleep. One slender tanned leg dangled over the side of the bed, snared by a tangle of white sheets. Her arm was buried under the pillow, and her silky hair now tousled by sleep, covered one naked shoulder. Dark lashes fanned her flushed cheek. Smiling, he walked into the bathroom and tested the shower, it was hot. The electricity was back on.

Dressed and with coffee in hand he walked through to his office. He looked across to Manhattan and saw his company logo blazing in the dawn light from the top of his New York hotel. Originally a disused warehouse, it had been Gramps' first, in a chain of hotels across the states. He had been one of the first to see the sense in converting derelict buildings into luxury hotels and apartments. His business acumen had been inherited from his own father, an immigrant from England. Grant had studied law at university before following his ancestors into real estate, and so far, he was doing them proud. He'd inherited their nose for a deal. He took a sip of black coffee watching New York's nocturnal inhabitants scurry home against the tide of early morning commuters and mulled over the dream which had seemed so real, it had woken him with a start, and left him tossing and turning unable to sleep. He was sure the dream had derived from his conversation with Belle about Barringham Hall. Like most dreams this one had made no sense. It had started with a derelict sandstone building, the epitome of eighteenth century wealth, situated somewhere in an English countryside. He'd been welcomed at the entrance, by the glamorous couple in the portraits. The front door, a solid oak, was weather bleached and held in place by one rusted hinge. As he walked through the entrance, the door was restored and the rusted hinges became gleaming brass. Each room, as he passed through it, was transformed into the Art Deco style of the designs found in Gramps' attic.

Draining his coffee cup, he set it down on the desk and picked up the blueprints. There, scrawled across the bottom in pen and ink was a signature he hadn't noticed before. It seemed familiar. He reached into his desk drawer and retrieved a petrol cigarette lighter. The lighter had been discovered wedged at the back of the drawer when the French Polisher had restored the desk. Grant had rather liked it, and although he didn't smoke, he'd kept it. Turning it around in his hand he saw clearly engraved in the silver, the name Myles Barringham. His memory had been correct, the name matched the signature. Who were you? Before he could give it any further thought, his phone pinged with an e-mail alert. 'Check this out,' it said. He had a list of agents who searched out suitable premises for renovation, but he couldn't tell who had sent this. He opened the attachment, curious to know why they'd thought he might be interested in an English property. His heart skipped a beat as he scrolled through the images. There on the screen was the magnificent but totally derelict building he'd seen in the dream. It was advertised as Meadow Bank Hall, Derbyshire, England - for sale by auction. He read through the spec three times. Every bit of his business acumen screamed at him white elephant, walk away. But his gut instinct, a sort of sixth sense that kicked in just before his best deals, screamed louder. He knew the building would be his.

Chapter Three

Saturday morning dawned bright and clear, the world refreshed and sparkling after a night of storms. Lydia jogged across the park, enjoying the sweet smell of damp earth. The terror of the night before had dimmed in the light of day. She made her way around the lake and mulled over what had happened. Common sense told her it was nothing more than shadows playing tricks. She'd simply flicked on the light switch too quickly and it had shorted the circuit. It was most probably something to do with static electricity in the air. Yet her intuitive side wouldn't let her mind rest. *You sensed something*, it insisted. *Admit it, you saw something.* She shook her head to clear the images crowding her mind. Gulping down the clean air, she put on a spurt and ran as hard as she could to escape her thoughts.

Dripping in sweat, she cut across the grass and ran down the path to the newsagents.

'Morning Mrs. T' she gasped, short of breath now that she'd stopped running. 'Lovely day isn't it. What a storm last night though, I thought my bedroom window was caving in at one point.'

'You're telling me. I decided to get up in the end and make a cup of tea. Thought I'd wait on the paper van, didn't want the papers getting wet. Good job I did. There I was standing in the shop doorway drinking my tea, rain rolling down the road in rivers, rivers it were, when a flash of white caught my eye over at that bus shelter. I thought it was a cat or something. But it was a spaniel. Look in that box,' she jerked her head towards the back of the counter. Curled up on a blanket and fast asleep, was a chocolate brown and white pup, his speckled snout just visible beneath one curly brown ear. Right on cue, the little mouth opened and a pink ribbon tongue unfurled into a yawn. Two beautiful almond shaped eyes blinked sleepily up at Lydia and her heart melted.

'He's beautiful,' she whispered, 'what are you going to do with him?'

'Take him to the dog's home I expect.'

'He's very young. I can take him home with me, at least until his owner claims him. Can you put a notice in your shop window? I'll contact the police and the dog shelters. I'd better take some food for him as well while I'm here.' Just at that moment the pup jumped out of the box and began running around in circles, sniffing the floor.

'Oh dear, we'd better be quick!' Lydia lifted the pup and placed him gently on the pavement. He looked up at her as if to say, mind your own business, and ran back into the shop to deposit a small puddle of amber liquid in front of the counter.

'Come on pup I think it's time we left,' and scooping him under her arm, she reached for the bag of shopping.

'I'll add that shopping to your account, shall I?' Mrs. T. shouted after Lydia's retreating figure.

Back home Lydia let the pup have a run around the garden before taking him upstairs to her flat. She made him a temporary bed from a large cardboard box and put in bowls of food and water. 'Try not to paddle in that while I'm gone,' she said, heading for the bathroom. After a quick shower, she finger-pressed her wayward curls into submission, and went downstairs to the shop.

She stood, as she did most mornings, surveying the Art Deco room with pride. The Twenties and Thirties had fascinated her from childhood. Now she possessed an impressive collection of artefacts, which she displayed to their best advantage, giving the shop an air of authentic opulence.

Pippa breezed in making the little bell over the door jingle merrily. With her usual abundance of energy, she bid Lydia a cheery good morning, and made straight for the counter, pressed play on the answer phone and flipped open the diary. Lydia watched her perform this daily routine with fondness. She had studied fashion alongside her at university before venturing into interior design and Pippa had been her obvious choice as a partner in the business.

Lydia's eyes continued to rove around the shop. They skimmed the chaise longue where ladies perched to try on shoes and the sumptuous arm chairs where bored husbands waited, then on to the changing rooms and their peacock blue curtains tied back with gold tassels. Eventually her eyes came to rest on the display of hats near the window. Designed by Pippa, it was an inspirational work of art. She shivered as her mind replayed the terror of the previous night.

'Shall I put the kettle on?' Pippa said, disturbing her reverie. 'Oh, did you alter my display?'

'No, didn't you?'

'No, not to worry I'll soon sort it out. It will have been a customer; they're always muddling things up. There, that's better,' she said, smoothing the felt on a wide brimmed cloche and setting it back in place. 'Lydia you've gone as white as a sheet, have you eaten yet?'

Lydia wrinkled her nose and shook her head.

'No, I thought not. Will scrambled eggs do?'

Ten minutes later, they were tucking into light fluffy eggs with hot buttered toast. They ate in the workroom with one ear listening out for the shop door.

'About your hat display. Something really weird happened last night,' Lydia said, and she proceeded to tell Pippa all about the moonlight and the shadows and how she'd discovered the hats had been tampered with after the light bulb exploded.

'Don't let the display get to you. Like I said, customers mess it up all the time. As for the shadows, I think your tired brain conjured them up. You must be exhausted covering Jenny's clients as well as your own. When does she get back from holiday?'

'Tomorrow,' Lydia said, stifling a yawn. 'She's back at work on Monday.'

'You sound worn out, I bet you'll be glad to hand over her workload.'

'That's not the problem. I can't sleep in this heat. Did you see the meteor shower last night? The sky was amazing. I've never seen so many stars.'

'Yes, I did see it. What about all those shooting stars? I've never seen one of those before, I made a wish, did you?'

Before Lydia could answer, the shop door crashed open with such force, that it knocked the bell clean off its hook. It clattered across the floor and was crushed under Pippa's foot as she stepped out of the workroom. The door was swinging back and forth in the sudden squall, but the shop was empty.

'False alarm, I can't have closed the door properly when I came in this morning. We'll need a new bell though,' she said, putting the crushed metal onto the table and picking up the empty plates. 'Don't bother taking these upstairs. I'll rinse them through in here. We'll need them for a sandwich at lunchtime anyway.'

'Good idea, now I'd better get on with the paperwork before the shop gets busy. I might bring the puppy's box down to the office, he'll be out of the way in there and I can keep an eye on him. Was he alright when you went upstairs?'

'Puppy?'

'Brown and white wriggly thing in a box in the living room.'

'You're kidding, where did that come from?'

'He came free with the morning paper.'

'That's the sleep deprivation talking. You're hallucinating.'

'I'm being serious. Mrs. T. at the newsagents rescued him from the storm. She was going to take him to the dogs' home, so I said I'd look after him until we find his owners. That's another thing I've to do this morning, contact the police and dog shelters.'

She stepped into the shop expecting it to be empty and came face to face with the most strikingly beautiful woman she had ever seen. The woman's hair, cropped into a sleek bob, shone like black silk beneath a tiny cloche hat, the perfect frame for her elfin features. Violet blue eyes studied Lydia with a level gaze, yet the hint of a smile tugged at one corner of her ruby mouth. Her shift dress, the same shade of tangy lemon as the hat, was made from a delicate crepe de chine and the low waist sat comfortably about her slim hips. Lydia was as much fascinated by the appearance of this vision as by the woman herself. There was an ethereal quality about her, a peaceful tranquillity and Lydia was transfixed. She suddenly realised she was holding her breath while unashamedly staring. Quickly collecting her thoughts, she introduced herself.

'Oh, I know who you are,' said the woman, dropping her gaze to idly trace a gloved finger along the edge of the glass counter. Then seemingly losing interest in its contents, she crossed the shop floor to inspect the display of hats. Lifting the wide brimmed cloche, she twirled it slowly, before returning it to its stand and moving on to inspect a display of silk gloves and shimmering evening bags from Lydia's private collection.

'Fascinating, so very fascinating, everything's just the same and yet... quite, quite different.' Abruptly she spun around as though suddenly remembering she wasn't alone, a slight tremor rippled through her body.

'Oh! But you don't know who I am,' said the woman, seemingly gathering her thoughts and walking towards Lydia with an outstretched hand.

'Please forgive my lapse in manners. My name is Lady Barringham, and I'm hoping you might make a gown for me. I wonder... since we're of a similar build, would you mind awfully, trying on a few gowns so that I might get an idea of a style to suit?'

Lydia had tried on at least a dozen dresses and she was beginning to lose her patience with the lovely Lady Barringham. Counting to ten, she blew a wayward curl from her eye, plastered a smile on her face and stepped through the changing room curtain.

'That's it, that's the line I'm looking for!' Lady Barringham leapt from the chair and began taking a selection of georgette scarves from a display. 'Now if we drape this one across like so and drop this one from the waist there, and gather this section here.'

As she looked in the mirror, Lydia was surprised to see how the splash of colour provided by the scarves added warmth to her skin and accentuated the green flecks in her hazel eyes. The overall effect was sensational.

'There!' declared Lady Barringham. 'A triumph, what do you say?'

'Oh absolutely. The contrast is stunning and these shades suit my fair colouring very well. But I think the blue would be a better choice for you. It will make a more striking contrast to your dark hair and emphasise the blue of your eyes.

Perhaps if you try on both dresses you'll see what I mean.'

Lady Barringham's eyes sparkled mischievously 'Ah, but you see this dress suits my requirements perfectly.'

Lydia changed into her own clothes then joined Lady Barringham at the counter. 'The dress should be ready for you by Monday afternoon, if that's convenient.'

'Perfect. My contact details,' she said, handing over a gilt-edged card and a cheque for the full amount.

'Thank you, do you want the dress to be delivered?'

'That won't be necessary,'

When Lydia looked up from writing the receipt, she was astonished to find that Lady Barringham had gone. It was then that she noticed the display. The hats had been switched again, in exactly the same way as the previous night.

The rest of the day was hectic. About four o'clock, there was a lull and they took the opportunity to grab a coffee. 'That's unusual,' Pippa said, picking up the guilt edged card.

'What's unusual?' Lydia asked, coming in from the garden with the pup under her arm.

'This,' she said, showing her the card. 'Have you ever seen a phone number as short as that? The printers must have missed some digits off.'

'That's Lady Barringham's. I didn't get chance to look at it earlier.' She turned it over in her hand, 'It looks like her taste in vintage extends to her calling cards. Barringham Hall, I've never heard of it, have you?'

'No. Let's dial the number.' Pippa reached for the phone. 'No luck, number not recognised. When's she coming back for the dress?'

'Monday afternoon and she's already paid for it, so we'd better make a start on those alterations.'

'Do you think she'll show?'

'I don't see why she wouldn't.

Chapter Four

On Monday, with Jenny back from holiday and Pippa in charge of the shop, Lydia took the pup to the vet's.

'Good morning,' Nick James said, standing in the doorway of the consulting room. Lydia looked up at him, and wondered if he'd paused there for effect, since the light from the window behind him had created a halo around his head. She was half expecting to hear a blast of the hallelujah chorus; instead she was momentarily blinded by a flash of unnaturally white teeth.

'You're next, Miss Lockwood!' The receptionist's voice boomed impatiently across the waiting room. She jumped up and followed him into the room.

'So, this little chap was found wandering? He seems in fairly-good shape after his ordeal. I'll give him some shots and wormers for now. Are you happy to keep him?'

'For as long as it takes.'

'Good, have you thought of a name for him?'

'Billy,' she said, without hesitation, although she had no idea why that particular name had suddenly sprung to mind.

'Good choice. Do you need a puppy crate for him to sleep in? I can lend you one of ours for now. Would you like me to drop it off on my way home?'

'Thank you, if you're sure it's no trouble that would be great.'

Staggering home with her arms full of food and chew toys, Lydia realised she was looking forward very much to another meeting with Nick James.

True to his word he arrived with the puppy crate after evening surgery. Lydia had a Bolognese sauce simmering on the hob. The bottle of red wine she'd used to spice it up stood open on the kitchen work top.

'Something smells good,' he said, setting the crate down. Billy, who was having a mad half hour charging around the apartment in bouncy circles, picked up one of his new toys and took it over to Nick to play tug of war.

'Would you like a glass of red wine or are you in a hurry?' she said.

'Would I ever? It's been a tough day. I was operating all afternoon, and it was my late surgery. I feel exhausted.'

'Then stay to dinner if you like, as a thank you for the loan of the puppy crate.'

'I never turn down an offer to be fed,' he laughed.

'Good, the sauce is about ready, I'll just set another place and put the pasta on to cook. Make yourself comfortable, there's an evening paper on the sofa.' She was pleased when he took himself off to the living room. She never liked people watching her cook.

They didn't linger over the meal, but by the time they were sitting on the sofa drinking coffee, the sun was setting and twilight's blush stained the room. Billy was snuggled up asleep in his crate, lulled by a soft breeze floating in through the French doors. Birds twittered in the trees settling in to roost, then stillness crept over the evening.

'It's so peaceful here, you have a beautiful home,' he said.

'Thank you, it's taken quite a while to get sorted. I was too involved in building up the business at first to even think about sorting out my living accommodation.'

'This is a lovely part of the country, what made you settle here?'

'Born and bred. I've never really wanted to live anywhere else. Of course, I went away to Uni, but I couldn't wait to get back. My parents decided to take early retirement, and emigrated to one of the Canary Islands around the time I graduated. When their house was sold, they offered me an early inheritance to help buy this business. It was an opportunity too good to miss, especially with the living accommodation above and being situated right in the heart of the village. It was a bit run down when I took it over, so I've spent more or less every waking hour turning it around.'

'What do you do in your spare time? I'll re-phrase that,' he laughed, 'social time?'

'I don't really,' she answered truthfully. 'Oh, I go out sometimes with Jenny and Pippa, but for the most part I'm working on designs in the evening.'

'There's an article here that might interest you,' he said, handing her the evening paper. 'Apparently, an American's bought Meadow Bank Hall and he's turning it into a hotel. It sounds as though the hall's in a pretty derelict state. The new owner boasts he can usually complete a refurbishment in less than six months but it's going to take more time to refurbish Meadow Bank. He's aiming for next year and planning to celebrate the opening with a Midsummer's Eve Ball, themed on the Roaring Twenties. Could be good for your business, you'll probably get quite a few dress orders.'

Intrigued, Lydia took the paper from him. The article went on to highlight some of the building's history and to explain how changes in society brought about by the First World War had forced the titled family to abandon their ancestral home. The building had been put to a variety of uses since then, but had remained empty for many years: eventually falling into decay. The article finished with a publicity plug for the hotel's opening event.

Putting the paper aside, she turned to face Nick. 'The article makes it sound a very exciting weekend. But in my experience these events are a bit of a disappointment.'

'What makes you say that?'

'Oh, they're usually lacking in authenticity. I bet the waitresses will be wearing token Charleston dresses to serve the meal, and afterwards a DJ will play a mega mix of Charleston music, before the disco takes over. It's just an excuse to get people into the hotel for the weekend, knowing they'll want a drink, so they'll have to book a room because they don't want to drink and drive.'

'That's a rather cynical point of view.'

'Put it down to experience.'

'I take it you won't be going then,' he laughed.

'I'll think about it. Anyway, how about you? Which did you choose first, the veterinary practice or the village?'

'Both actually. When I was a child my parents used to rent a farm cottage here for the summer.'

'The Bryson's farm? It's gone now. It was knocked down to build new housing.'

'So I've discovered. Well it was Mr Bryson who first fired up my interest in animals. I would follow him around the farm all day. Then in the evening we'd walk through the meadow down to the river searching out birds and wild creatures.'

'The Bryson's still live locally you know, you could go and see them.'

'Yes, I know, Mr. Bryson brought his dog into the surgery. I was invited to high tea. Mrs Bryson makes the best scones I've ever tasted.'

Just then Billy emerged sleepily from his crate and Lydia scooped him up and carried him through the French doors and down the steps to the garden. Nick followed her saying 'Mr. Bryson gave me a collie pup for my tenth birthday, a little ball of black and white fur. I was completely besotted. I think that was the moment I decided to become a vet. We had a long and happy relationship together...' For a moment, he seemed lost for words, deep in thought staring into the distance, somewhere out of reach to her, before suddenly saying in barely a whisper, 'unlike others I can think of...unfortunately.'

Billy, having completed his duty, was chasing a moth attracted by the security lighting. Running too fast for his legs, he went head over heels landing splay-footed with one ear forward and one ear back. The pup's comical antics immediately lightened Nick's mood, but Lydia was still quite relieved when he left shortly afterwards.

'Phew Billy,' she said, lifting the pup into her arms, 'Mr Vet might be gorgeous, but I'll bet he's carrying a lot of emotional baggage.'

Chapter Five

It was a week later that the bank returned Lady Barringham's cheque. It was apparently a bankers' draft, which hadn't been in circulation since well before World War II.

'I thought it was some sort of personalised designer cheque,' Lydia laughed. 'It's a wonder she's not been back to collect the dress before the truth was discovered.'

'What do you think she was up to?'

'I've really no idea. The whole thing's a bit weird. When I first saw her in the shop, I thought for a ridiculous moment that she'd simply wandered in from the Nineteen-Twenties. Take her dress for instance, those materials were widely used decades ago, but fabrics of that compound are rare these days. Modern technology can produce a similar product more cheaply. And her hat and shoes, well they looked brand new.'

'So what?' shrugged Pippa, 'Perhaps they'd never been worn?'

'Maybe, but you'd think the fabric and colour would have deteriorated to some extent. Oh, well, at least we've still got the dress. We can put it out for sale. I doubt very much Lady Barringham will put in another appearance.'

Lydia's assumption had been correct. The dress hadn't been collected, and it remained all but forgotten, concealed amongst the other dresses hanging on a rail in the shop.

Towards the end of the summer, Lydia was driving home from a meeting with clients, when Billy, who'd been cooped up in the car for much of the afternoon, began whining. 'Alright Billy Boy, I'll stop for a walk. I could do with stretching my legs anyway.' She pulled up in a leafy lay-by fringed by woodland and opened the boot of the car. Billy jumped out and disappeared into the woods. She followed, listening for sounds of him thrashing about in the undergrowth. The absolute silence was eerie. She stooped to pick up a dog lead which someone had dropped and walked back to hang it over the gate. Returning to the spot where Billy had vanished, she stood a while surprised that the dog hadn't come bounding back to her by now. The trees sporting their late summer foliage presented a thick canopy and dappled sunlight filtered through making dancing patterns on a carpet of fallen leaves. She walked deeper into the woods whistling and calling his name. She stopped to listen, the silence was all encompassing now. A chill ran down her spine, she felt sure someone was watching. A twig cracked and she spun around, flinching as a crow flew at her from a bush, it veered off just short of contact and soared upwards through the canopy. She scanned the woods, every direction seemed unfamiliar, the trees and shrubs were dense; she had totally lost her bearings. Then she spotted a path partially obscured by undergrowth and she set off running, dodging the low branches and pushing aside the ferns blocking her path. 'Billy! Here boy,' she shouted as loud as she could. Her mouth was too dry to whistle. She ran on, her heart pounding. Nettles mottled her legs but she didn't feel their sting. Then a bramble snagged her foot and she landed spread eagle in the dirt. The fall brought her to her senses. She got up brushing her hands and knees. No cuts, only bruises. She looked about, no-one was following.

Before long, she'd reached open shrub land and there, she could see Billy in the distance leaping up and down making his way through the rough terrain. Relief washed over her, and she bent double, resting her hands on her knees to catch her breath.

By the time she'd crossed the shrub land, Billy had disappeared again and she'd reached the boundary of cultivated land. Making her way deeper into the grounds, she realised they were the type of landscaped gardens usually associated with stately homes. Oh, god, I hope they don't have an ornamental lake. A vision of Billy thrashing about among the lilies flashed before her.

'Where the hell are you?' she said, in a stage whisper. 'Billy, Billy, here boy!' she shouted at the top of her voice.

'Is this the young scamp you're after, Miss?'

Spinning around she saw an elderly man stooped to almost her height, holding Billy's collar in one gnarled hand and his cap in the other. He was smiling kindly, his merry brown eyes creasing up at the corners of his weather-beaten face. A wide grin revealed absent teeth. Returning his infectious smile, she noticed with horror the tell-tale pattern of muddy paw prints splattered across his chest.

'Yes,' she gasped, 'thank you, he's my young scamp, but he's never run away from me before like this. I'm really sorry about your shirt. I hope he hasn't caused any other damage.'

'Not to the garden he ain't,' the man answered, pushing back his shirt sleeve to reveal a sinewy forearm, 'but if you don't mind my saying so, Miss, best not let the gamekeeper know you was out on them moors with him off the lead. There's plenty of young grouse about. Dog could've disturbed 'em you see. You'd best put him on his lead now, and leave by the front gates.'

'Oh, but my car's parked in a lay-by way over there,' she said, nodding her head in the general direction as she struggled to get a wriggling Billy back on his lead.

'You parked in Meadow Bank Lane?' he asked, stooping to re-tie the string around the knee of his corduroy trousers.

'That's right, how did you know?'

'It borders onto our land, if you walk down the driveway and turn right at the end, then carry on for half a mile, you'll come to your car right enough. It's deceptive walking the way you came, the path meanders and that. You take the road way now. It's more direct see, so it'll be quicker.' Then straightening the gauze cravat at his throat and wriggling his cap to a snug fit he turned and walked away, disappearing somewhere amidst the foliage. Lydia watched the space where he had been.

As she reached the far end of the gardens the house came into view. A much grander building than she'd expected. Meadow Bank Lane, the old man had said. Of course, this must be Meadow Bank Hall. She could hear jazz music playing through the open window. The glass sparkled, reflecting the bright sunlight. The drapes framing the windows looked full and luxurious. The brass fittings on the front door were buffed to perfection and the steps leading up to it had been scrubbed clean, and more surprisingly, looked freshly donkey stoned.

I was wrong about this place, she thought, noticing the attention to period detail. They must have cracked on with the refurbishment. Mindful of the gamekeeper, she didn't linger to discover more, and following the old man's directions, soon found her car.

Chapter Six

The following day when the postman arrived, he handed Lydia an embossed, gilt-edged, cream envelope. The flap had been secured with sealing wax. 'You'll have to sign for this one if you don't mind. I'm afraid there's a charge for the postage on account of the stamp being obsolete. It's strange that. Nobody at the sorting office has ever seen the likes of it before. You never know, it might be worth a bob or two, you could end up getting more than your money back.' And then hitching his post bag on to his shoulder he strode out of the shop, whistling tunelessly.

Lydia tucked the post under her arm and still holding the letter walked through to the office. She turned it over in her hands before opening it. There was something familiar about the stationery. Using a paper knife, she slit open the top so as not to disturb the seal and carefully pulled out the contents. It was an invitation to the Midsummer's Eve Ball. 'Hey come and look at this,' she called.

Jenny studied the invitation, 'Bit previous aren't they,' she said.

'Perhaps they're sending out early invitations to local businesses as a promotion,' Pippa suggested. 'If they've done their homework, they'll know we're likely to be interested. Bit of a cheek about the postage though, unless that's part of the promotion. You know, turn up to claim your refund... I wonder if the visit from Lady Barringham was part of a publicity stunt. That invitation looks a lot like her business card.'

'Look at the venue,' Jenny pointed out, 'It isn't the Meadow Bank Hall, it's Barringham Hall.'

'That's the same address as Lady Barringham's card. Perhaps the owner has changed the name of the building now it's to be a hotel. What do you make of this? Whoever sent it has used sealing wax and stamped it with a crest.'

'We might discover that the mysterious Lady Barringham lives there after all,' Jenny laughed.

'I doubt it, anyway, while we're on the subject of the Midsummer's Eve Ball, I've an idea I want to run past you. I've been thinking about it ever since Nick James pointed it out. The theme is to be the Roaring Twenties. Do you think our customers would prefer to buy from us, rather than pay to hire fancy dress?'

'I'm sure they would,' Jenny agreed. 'It's the grand opening of the hotel. All the local dignitaries and press will be there. That ruin of a building has been a landmark for so many years, I shouldn't be at all surprised if a television crew turns up to film the transformation. So yes, great idea, let's go for it. Absolutely amazing publicity for us.'

'Good, I thought you'd agree. Shall we put a full-page advertisement in the paper offering a ten percent discount? If we take a risk and run up a batch of our best sellers, I think it will be a risk worth taking. What do you think Pippa? The bulk of the workload will fall on your shoulders.'

'The work's no problem, I can draft in the casual machinists from the village. They're always pleased of some extra hours. I think though that we should personalise the finishing touches, to make each dress appear unique. My only other concern is that the refurbishment hasn't even started yet. There's many a slip between cup and lip, as my gran is always reminding me.'

'Well it looks about finished to me.'

'How do you know?'

'I saw it yesterday when I parked on Meadow Bank Lane to give Billy a run. Do you know those woods? They're a bit spooky. Beautiful, but definitely spooky. Billy dashed off and I'd no idea which way he'd gone, I bumbled about until I'd completely lost my bearings. Fortunately, I found a path hidden by ferns, leading onto shrub land. When I caught up with Billy, he'd crossed over it and gone into the grounds of Meadow Bank Hall.'

'Wait a minute, that doesn't make sense,' Jenny said.

'Would now be a good time to make some tea?' Pippa asked, edging out of the office.

'Good idea. What doesn't make sense?' Lydia said, relaxing back into her chair.

'Billy running off for a start, he never usually leaves your side. But what I really mean, is that those woods back onto the Meadow Bank housing estate, they're usually full of kids on bikes and rope swings. Are you sure you parked on Meadow Bank Lane?'

'Positive, the gardener who'd caught Billy told me not to let him run about in the shrub land because of the young grouse. Then he directed me past the hall and back to the lane.'

'I can't think what shrub land you mean. The housing estate is between the woods and the hall. There's a golf club nearby. You weren't bumbling about in their roughs, were you?'

'Credit me with a bit more intelligence,' she said, rolling her eyes. 'And I'm telling you, there definitely wasn't a housing estate.'

'Well, I'll bet you a tenner there is.'

'Right you're on. Shall we go tonight? Hey Pippa, how do you fancy joining us for a nosy at the newly refurbished Meadow Bank Hall Hotel?'

'Great idea,' she said, putting the tea tray down on the desk. 'We could go to The Crown for dinner afterwards.'

They set off immediately after the shop closed and Lydia parked her car in the same lay-by as the day before. The dog lead she'd found was still dangling over the gate where she'd left it. Once inside the woods, Billy walked close to heel, which was just as well, because exactly as Jenny had predicted the area was swarming with bicycles. The carpet of fallen leaves had vanished, buried under a sea of mud and makeshift ramps, cobbled together to make a BMX circuit.

The biggest surprise was stepping out of the gloom into the piercing sunlight reflecting off the windows opposite. The stark concrete buildings looked neatly uniformed in the distinctive design of post-war local authority housing. And their carefully tended gardens, though bursting with vibrant colours, did nothing to soften their severity.

Lydia stood at the kerb, hand on forehead to shield her eyes from the glare as she looked up and down the road. 'I must have come out of the woods in a different place. There was just a vast open space yesterday, not a privet hedge in sight.'

'This is definitely the Meadow Bank housing estate,' Jenny assured her. 'It spreads beyond the woods in each direction. Come on, we have to walk through the estate to reach Meadow Bank Hall.'

'How come you know so much about this area?'

'I once lived here.'

The centre of the estate, formed around a patch of green, held a rather nostalgic atmosphere with children out playing hopscotch and tag. Two older girls turned a length of washing line, while several children skipped together, chanting to the rhythm of their pounding feet. Friendly banter passed back and forth over the hedges from keen gardeners trimming already immaculate privet. And as the merry tune of an ice-cream van faded into the distance, the evidence of its recent visit was plastered across the faces of the younger children.

'Look, there's Meadow Bank Hall!' Jenny pointed out, as they came to a standstill alongside a road of fast moving traffic. Lydia's heart sank. Up until now she'd convinced herself that she had come out of a different part of the woods yesterday. But there was no denying that the building across the road with its majestic façade was definitely one and the same. Except now it was barricaded and derelict. Not even the surrounding land bore any resemblance.

'I can't work this out. I know I parked the car in the same spot as yesterday, because that red dog lead I'd picked up was still hanging from the gate.'

'Yes, that was still there today,' Pippa said. 'Shall we walk around the perimeter to see what else you can spot?' They waited for the pedestrian lights to change then dashed across the road. As soon as they reached the far kerb, Billy wrenched the lead from Lydia's hand and with his nose to the ground began sniffing around the perimeter fence. Then he let out an excited yelp and began scrabbling frantically; his front paws successfully working loose a joint in the fencing.

He wriggled his busy little body through and ran off at top speed disappearing around the back of the hall.

'What on earth's got into that dog?'

'I don't know, but I'm game to follow him if you are,' Jenny said, squeezing through the gap. Lydia slipped in easily behind her.

'Hang about a minute!' Pippa shouted, looking down at her ample bosom. 'I've more equipment to manoeuvre than you two!'

'Breath out,' Jenny laughed. 'Come on we'll pull you through if you get stuck.'

'I hope we don't get done for trespassing,' Pippa said, managing to squeeze through the gap in the fencing at last. 'And I hope there aren't any guard dogs.'

'Don't worry. I expect they'd have attacked Billy by now if there were. I wonder where he's got to.' The light was fading fast as Lydia approached the hall. The row of stone gargoyles stared down forlornly from their perch under the eaves. Pieces of nose and the occasional tooth had corroded away, where before they had looked perfectly ghoulish. The previously sparkling windows were now cracked, held together by cobwebs. The once welcoming door dangled pathetically from one rusted hinge, weather bleached and lifeless. Through the crack, Lydia could hear Billy snuffling around, his tail thumping excitedly, his claws pattering against the floor as though greeting someone familiar. The dark memory of dancing in the moonlight at the shop flooded her senses. And with it came the same peculiar feeling of something, someone, watching her, and yes… that was it, an overwhelming feeling of anticipation. Frowning, she called Billy, relieved when he came to heel immediately. Stooping to pick up his lead she saw he'd trailed sooty paw prints from behind the door and all the way down the steps. 'What have you been up to?' she said, stroking the dog's silky head.

'Come on Lydia,' Pippa said, coming to stand beside her and wrapping an arm around her shoulders. 'We'll need to get going if we want to get to The Crown before they stop serving.'

The food at The Crown proved to be every bit as delicious as they remembered. They drank their coffee beside a log fire enjoying its warmth; the evening had turned surprisingly chilly.

'It doesn't look like Meadow Bank Hall will be transformed into a hotel any time soon,' Jenny said, draining her cup. 'I even wonder if it'll be ready in time for the opening.'

'Doesn't look like they'll be open in the next year to be honest' Pippa agreed. 'What do you think Lydia? You've been quiet all through dinner.'

'Me? Oh, I think I must be going mad!'

Jenny's hysterical laughter ricocheted around the old inn and a man reading quietly in the corner lowered his newspaper to glower at her over the top of his reading glasses.

'Come off it,' Jenny said, 'You're the sanest person I know. In fact, a bit more vivid imagination might do you the world of good. So, what did this gardener look like? Anything like Lady Chatterley's?' That sent Lydia off into peals of laughter, causing the man to rattle his paper loudly. Pippa turned to pull a face in his direction, but he was busy reading.

'No, nothing like it! He looked like the Crooked Man, you know the one from the nursery rhyme. But he had kind brown eyes and a lovely wrinkly old face. I can't think how old he must be, but he was dressed in really old fashioned clothes.'

'How do you mean?'

'Well he was wearing corduroy trousers, but they were tied with string just below the knee. His flat cap was made of cloth and round his neck was some sort of cravat scarf which looked like it had been knitted with string.'

'How delightfully eccentric! You didn't fall and bump your head in the woods, did you?'

'Very funny! Although... Can you come up with a better explanation? Because I can't.'

Chapter Seven

Life pretty much returned to normal after that. Then in the spring a feature about the Meadow Bank Hall Hotel appeared in the evening paper. The grand opening was to go ahead as planned with the Nineteen-Twenties themed, Midsummer's Eve Ball. Lydia advertised the readymade dresses offering a ten percent discount and the response was beyond anything she could have imagined. Pippa offered the local machinists full time hours to fulfil the orders on time.

On the day of the ball the three of them had intended to travel to the hotel together, but Lydia was delayed by a client, so Jenny and Pippa set off without her.

By the time she had appeased the client and secured the building, she was running later than anticipated. Just as she was about to pull the door closed, she noticed the dress that Lady Barringham had commissioned sticking out from the rack. In a snap decision, she made a grab for it. Folding it over her arm, she set the burglar alarm and pulled the door closed, locking it securely.

After driving for an hour, navigating the twisting country lanes at top speed, she was just beginning to doubt the Sat Nav, when she spotted the sign for the hotel.

'At last!' she exclaimed, turning into the sweeping driveway and bringing the car to a halt with a resounding crunch of tyres. She grabbed her belongings from the boot and ran up the stone steps.

The door was opened by a stereotypical Edwardian butler, and waiters in similar attire were handing out cocktails from silver trays. She began to feel quite optimistic that the hotelier might have organized an authentic event after all. But while waiting to check in, she had plenty of time to scrutinize the hotel's interior and her high hopes were dashed by the minimalist design. She went straight to her room, and after a quick shower styled her hair. Then, feeling exhausted and with time to spare, she lay down on the bed to rest for a few moments…

She woke with a start and groaned when she saw the time. It was after eight o'clock; she had missed the pre-dinner drinks altogether. Dashing to the wardrobe, she grabbed the nearest dress and dragged it over her head. As she left, she checked her appearance in the door mirror and realised she was wearing Lady Barringham's dress. With no time to change, she quickly made her way along the corridor and down the sweeping staircase.

Halfway down, she stopped so abruptly that she had to grab the banister to prevent herself from tumbling the rest of the way. Gone was the minimalist interior, the scene below held all the opulence of the Orient Express. Enormous white globes suspended by chrome rods illuminated the foyer. An arrangement of fragrant lilies swamped a Ruhlman cabinet, their image reflected in the cabinet's high gloss. A second cabinet hosted two bronze figurines posed in precarious stance, each balancing a globe light in the palm of her hand.

Wooden parquet flooring now replaced the high gloss tiles, and a geometric patterned carpet of peacock blue and burnt orange was fastened to the stairs by brass rods. Heavy drapes less patterned, but picking out the colours of the carpet, framed the long window at the end of the landing, and in front of the window a chaise longue had been strategically placed, to sit and enjoy the gardens and glorious countryside beyond. They were the same gardens she realised, where she had found Billy with the eccentric gardener. The drab Meadow Bank housing estate was nowhere to be seen.

In the hallway to the right of the staircase, enormous mirrors reflected light onto another vast array of lilies swamping a glossy table, the partner to the Ruhlman cabinet. Their heavy scent was intoxicating.

Positioned in front of a giant potted palm, his back ramrod straight, stood an officious looking butler greeting guests and checking names from a leather-bound book. The hotel staff, she reasoned, must be magicians to have replaced carpets and chandeliers in the short space of time since her arrival, but how on earth had they replaced the wall and floor coverings. She couldn't begin to comprehend the change in the view from the window. Unless of course it was a holographic projection. She hadn't paused long enough to study it.

Hovering on the stairs in bewilderment, she jumped at the touch on her elbow.

'I say, are you feeling quite well?'

She turned and a pair of vivid blue eyes met her gaze, their mischievous twinkle belied the concern in the man's voice. A strong jaw defined his classical good looks and in the shimmering lamplight his hair shone gold.

'I… Yes, thank you, it's just the décor, it took me by surprise.'

'Rather daring for this old place don't you think? Quite up to the minute.' He was still holding her arm and standing so close she could feel his breath on her cheek.

'I'm sorry, what do you mean?'

'The décor, you said it was surprising. I presume that means you like it.'

'No. I mean yes. Oh, dear, what I really mean is, do you know how they managed to change it so quickly. Do you suppose the view from the landing window is a holographic projection or a green screen or something?'

'I'm frightfully sorry, I haven't the foggiest idea what you're talking about. I say, you do look a trifle queer. Here, let's get you down these stairs before you fall down them,' he said, offering his arm with an exaggerated bow, 'Myles Barringham at your service.'

'Why thank you,' she giggled nervously. 'Lydia Lockwood, damsel in distress,' and taking his arm, they descended the stairs together. She reached the last step just as her legs gave way and she landed on her bottom with a thump. 'What did you say your name was?'

'Myles Barringham.'

'Yes, that's what I thought you said.' She stayed sitting on the step while a waiter brought her a glass of water. She fervently hoped that Lady Barringham wouldn't make a scene when she saw her wearing 'the' dress, which she realised with growing dismay, must have been ordered to wear to this ball.

'Here drink this,' encouraged Myles. 'It'll put some roses back into your cheeks.' She took a big gulp of the water, only to discover that it was laced with gin. When she had eventually stopped coughing, she looked up at Myles who was smiling down at her, his blue eyes twinkling mischievously. She thought again how incredibly handsome he was, immaculately dressed in black tie.

'I'm so sorry, I've made you late for dinner,' she managed to say. 'Lady Barringham must be wondering what's happened to you.' For a split second the warmth in his eyes faded. Then smiling he said, 'I can assure you, she will not overly concern herself regarding my whereabouts.'

Lydia decided she'd better make herself scarce, just to be on the safe side, she didn't want to get into an argument over a dress nor did she want to become embroiled in his domestic affairs.

'Right,' she said, planting a hand on each thigh and getting to her feet, 'thank you so much for your help, I'm sure I've wasted quite enough of your time already, I'm meeting friends so I …'

'Madam,' the somber looking butler stepped forward interrupting her with a slight bow 'May I enquire as to your name?'

He searched through his guest list and couldn't find a match. He also checked under Pippa, Jenny and the shop's name. Embarrassingly aware of Myles eyes upon her, she could feel a sick sort of panic beginning to rise from the pit of her stomach, but he simply stepped forward and offered his arm. 'Obviously, some clerical error,' he said calmly, 'why not dine at my table and look for your friends afterwards.'

Not wishing to make a further spectacle of herself she took his arm and followed him into the dining room. As the chair was held out for her to sit to the table, she looked in amazement at the dining room's sumptuous furnishings and the careful attention to period detail. The great banqueting table, which she presumed was made up of several smaller tables pushed together, was covered with an enormous snow white Irish linen table cloth. The vast floral arrangement, which made it difficult to see her dinner companions across the table, was of a late Edwardian style, as was the dinner service, the crystal glasses and the solid silver cutlery. Turning her glass around before sipping the wine, she wondered where they'd found such a large matching collection of vintage tableware. She couldn't believe that a hotel, or anyone, for that matter would set items of such quality out for public use.

With this puzzling thought she focused on the diners. Without exception, each one was the epitome of the Twenties era, their hair was styled to perfection. Not only the women either. She stifled a giggle as she noticed a portly middle aged man with a Marcel wave comb over, his heavily waxed moustache twirled to a lethal point. He could take someone's eye out with that, she thought, and the giggle escaped as she imagined him leaning in, to whisper into his unsuspecting companion's ear. They must be a part of some sort of Roaring Twenties appreciation society, she decided. Even so, it was unusual to find such overall high standard of fancy dress. Then another thought struck her, out of all the multitude of orders she and her team had produced, she didn't recognise even one of her own or Pippa's designs being worn here tonight. Her train of thought led her to wondering where her two colleagues had got to, she couldn't see them anywhere in the

51

dining room. Her thoughts were interrupted just then, by the arrival of dinner.

'This food tastes so amazing, it must be organic. What do you think?'

'Organic? I'm blowed if I know what you mean.'

'You know, grown without pesticides and stuff. I wonder who their supplier is. If they're local, I'd like to use them.'

Myles looked puzzled for a moment and took his time considering her question, then the penny seemed to drop. 'Oh, I see what you mean, well we're pretty much self-sufficient here, what with the estate and everything.'

'This estate? But I thought all the pasture land had been sold off. The Meadow Bank housing estate is built on it.'

'Good Lord!' he exploded, 'Jolly fast workers those builder chappies. Rode round the estate myself only this morning, everything was ship shape and tickerty boo then. No sheep in the meadow or cows in the corn, what!' She knew he was teasing her. Oh, well, just play the game, she thought. He's obviously enjoying playing his part up to the hilt pretending to be the Lord of the Manor.

After exchanging a few words with her fellow diners, Lydia quickly realised that everyone else appeared to be play acting too. Definitely a Twenties appreciation society she thought, everyone's pretending to be living in the

Roaring Twenties and acting out the character to match their costume. She decided to get into the swing of things. Her dress was perfect for a well to do young lady, 'A bright young thing' - a Flapper!

After dinner, there was dancing and party games, the live band was sensational and the lack of amplification allowed the conversation to flow. A Statue dance was the first, and Lydia found she could join in quite easily. It was like playing musical statues in couples. Next the band leader announced a dance entitled 'A hiking we will go' Myles explained the basics, which involved making two lines, men in one line, girls in the other, facing each other.

'You have to sing the words:
A hiking we will go,
A hiking we will go,
We'll feel the breeze all around our knees, no matter if it snows!

Now the top couple will gallop sideways up and down the centre of the rows three times. Then make an arch, which everyone follows through and then the next couple takes a turn at galloping up and down the rows and so forth.'

The dance proved to be more energetic than she'd imagined, and she was just getting her breath back, when the first game was announced and once more the men and women were split into two teams at opposite sides of the room.

'Catch Your Mate. How on earth do you play that game?'

'You mean you've never played it?' the young woman standing next to her sounded incredulous. 'Why, it's the highlight of the evening. We girls get to pick the partner of our choice, rather than standing on the edge of the room hoping a tall handsome man will ask you to dance, instead of a short one with two left feet.'

Looking at the slender height of her companion, Lydia realised she probably did have difficulty in finding a partner to suit.

'Do you see those curtain rings on the table over there? Well you must grab one of the chaps from the line, run with him to the table, put a curtain ring over both your thumbs joining them together, and run back to your seat with him. The winner gets to keep her partner for the rest of the game, the losers have another go at choosing a mate until everyone is paired up. I've got my eye on that chap over there, the one with the glorious wavy auburn hair. He's got heavenly chocolate brown eyes.'

'Ah, it's a bit like a lady's excuse me then.' Lydia said, 'My nan used to tell me about those.'

'Pardon me?' the young woman asked distractedly, drooling over her 'dreamboat' as she'd nicknamed him.

'On your marks, ladies,' announced the band leader, 'get set, and go!' Lydia made a dash for the nearest chap and just as she reached for him, Myles shouldered him out of the way and made a grab for her. The thwarted man took it all in good fun, feigning his disappointment. Myles and Lydia raced to her seat, making it back in the nick of time. A waiter brought cold drinks to the table and they sipped them watching the hilarity spiral until the band leader announced the Charleston. A huge cheer went up and everyone rushed on to the dance floor.

After two more dances, they made their way to the edge of the floor. 'Wow, Myles,' she gasped. 'You're really good at the Charleston. Most men don't seem to be able to dance at all, let alone do the Charleston.'

'It's the latest craze don't you know! All my friends are doing it.' She was about to say the Charleston has been around for almost a hundred years, when someone whisked her back onto the dance floor. She was having such a wonderful time, she suddenly remembered she'd forgotten all about Jenny and Pippa. She was just contemplating what to do about them, when Myles cut in on her partner, and danced her out onto the terrace.

'Midsummer's Eve, a night of mysteries and magic. Do you believe in magic, Lydia? In wishes on shooting stars and love at first sight?' He was holding her very close she could feel his breath warm against her ear. A shiver ran down her spine as she recalled her secret wish. Curious at his choice of words she leaned back to look up at him and his eyes seemed to be burning into her, reading her thoughts, daring her to bare her soul. Moonlight flooded the terrace casting shadows and he suddenly gathered her into his arms as though he'd never let her go, and then gently he began to sway in time to the music. The elusive fragrance of honeysuckle, sensual and intoxicating filled the night air and she closed her eyes surrendering to his embrace.

'Come on,' he said, abruptly breaking the spell. 'I want to show you my latest and most favourite toy.' And leading her by the hand, he took her to what once must have been a stable block. He pulled open the doors, and there shining in the moonlight stood a bright blue Kissel Gold Bug Speedster sports car.

'My goodness it's perfect,' she whispered. 'Wherever did you get it restored?'

'Restored? It's hot foot from the factory, only 1000 miles on the clock. I ordered it when I was over in the States, had it shipped back.' He walked around to the passenger door and opened it. 'Hop in old bean, I'll take you for a spin.'

The rush of cold air felt wonderful against her skin after the hot interior of the hotel. With the wind tousling her hair, they sped across the estate and along twisting country lanes. It felt like they were chasing after the night and away from morning; secretly hoping to prolong the magical evening. But all too soon the night was drawing to its close, the first light appeared over the eastern horizon and an early bird began his call.

'Hang on a mo,' Myles said. 'Let me garage the pride and joy, then I'll walk you back.' At the door to her room, he reached for her hand and brushing his lips against her finger tips, he said, 'Farewell sweet Lydia, I'll see you in your dreams,' Then he turned and walked away.

'Don't you mean I'll see you in *my* dreams?' she called after his retreating figure, but he was already out of ear shot. As she watched him walk away, he seemed to walk on past the staircase and fade from view. Smiling sleepily, she made a mental note to visit an optician.

Persistent hammering filtered through Lydia's dreams and for a moment she couldn't work out where she was. Still half asleep, she padded to the door. The second she opened it, her friends burst in.

'Where on earth did you get to last night? We waited ages for you in the bar and left a message with the Maître d'. Didn't he give it to you? Why are you still in your glad rags by the way?' Jenny said, walking over to the window and lifting the voile curtain to check out the view.

'Wasn't the food appalling?' Pippa groaned as though she'd been poisoned. 'And what about the band, they couldn't play a note in tune!'

'No, they were so old they could hardly lift their instruments,' Jenny laughed.

'Slow down a bit,' Lydia winced holding her head. 'I've only just woken up. Here sit on the bed for a minute while I use the bathroom. Then I'll tell you what happened.'

They listened patiently to her version of the evening. Then Pippa stood up and walked over to the kettle and Jenny slipped an arm across Lydia's shoulders. 'You were dreaming darling,' she said soothingly. 'You've been working so hard while I was away.'

'But it was all so vivid. It wasn't like a dream at all. Well not like any I've ever had before!'

'Here drink this. It'll perk you up a bit,' Pippa said, giving Lydia a cup of coffee.

After she'd showered and dressed, she was convinced she'd slept right through the night and dreamed up the whole thing. It's ever since I made that stupid wish on the shooting star, she thought, it's haunting my subconscious.

Sure enough, when she went down to breakfast, the modern interior of the hotel was just the same as it had been when she'd arrived.

'Hurry up, slow coach!' Jenny said, coming up behind and linking arms, 'they stop

58

serving breakfast at ten.' Walking into the minimalist dining room, Lydia was struck by the stark contrast between this room and the ornate one she'd dreamed of the previous night. Her cheeks dimpled as she remembered the hilarious party games she'd played and how close Myles had held her dancing in the moonlight. He was the most amazing man she'd ever met.

The next thought struck her like a physical blow. She'd just met the man of her dreams. Unfortunately, he belonged in her dreams.

For the rest of the day, the girls joined in the scheduled activities. But Lydia felt little enthusiasm and was glad she was the spare in a game of mixed doubles. Lunch was followed by croquet on the lawn, and the day finished up with afternoon tea on the terrace.

Relieved the tedious day had finally ended, Lydia left the other two lingering over their tea and set off to her room to pack her bags. At the foot of the stairs she looked up to see Myles smiling down at her from the landing, his blue eyes twinkling mischievously. Before she could react, he'd turned and walked off along the landing in the same direction he'd taken the previous night.

Shouting his name, she ran after him as fast as she could and reached the landing just in time to see a door at the end of the corridor closing silently. She rattled the door knob, but it wouldn't budge. She banged loudly on the door shouting his name.

'Excuse me Madam,' said a hotel porter, coming up behind and trying to attract her attention. 'This part of the building is out of bounds to guests.'

'Well one of the guests just went in there and I need to speak to him, it's very important.' Her mind was in a complete whirl. She'd let her friends convince her that she'd been dreaming. Now that she'd seen him again, the memories of last night flooded back in vivid detail and she felt confused. Her pulse pounded in her ears and her head ached terribly. Turning to the door again, she hammered her fists against it with all her might.

'Madam, I must insist you stop banging, you're disturbing the other guests. This part of the hotel is unoccupied, none of the staff has a key and I can assure you no one can get in. You've seen for yourself that the door's locked.'

Reluctantly she turned away. All at once the need to escape the building was overwhelming and she quickly packed her bags and checked out.

Driving along the motorway, she pressed her foot down hard on the accelerator and opened the windows, hoping the blast of cold air might clear her head.

She was feeling much calmer when she reached the village. As she pulled into her allocated parking place, she was surprised to see Nick James standing outside her shop.

'Great timing,' he said, 'I was wondering if you fancied a walk by the river then a bite to eat at the Fox and Duck.'

'Do you know,' she replied, 'I would absolutely love that,' And she meant it.

They collected Billy from the dog minder and then walked through the woods and along the tow path to give him a run before settling in the beer garden. The river flowed silkily by, shades of green and blue reflected in its glass surface. The undercurrent was strong in places, making the ducks perform a comical dance, frantically paddling their little webbed feet trying to stay on the spot and darting backwards as the current won. Then with their bills thrust determinedly forwards, they'd flap and splash their way back up river, only to start their performance all over again. Watching them, Lydia and Nick laughed out loud and Billy barked excitedly wanting to join in the fun. The food was delicious and the conversation easy. Nick was a handsome man, and this evening there seemed to be no trace of the previous tension in him.

As evening faded into night, lights glowed along the river bank. Their reflection twinkling in the water reminded Lydia of dancing in the moonlight with Myles.

'Here, you're shivering, put this around your shoulders.' Nick said, offering his jacket.

'Thank you. It's been a lovely evening but a hectic weekend. If you don't mind, I'd like to head off home now.'

They walked back along the tow path in companionable silence, until Nick, noticing she was lost in thought, said, 'Penny for them?'

Looking up at him, she studied his face for a good few moments before shrugging her shoulders and saying. 'Oh, what the hell. Look, I'm going to tell you about something that happened to me last night at the hotel and you may think I'm completely mad, or you might agree with my friends, that I fell asleep and dreamed the whole thing. But either way here goes…'

When she'd finished speaking, Nick didn't laugh as she'd thought he might, instead he offered some practical suggestions. 'I agree with Jenny and Pippa that you must have fallen asleep, but I also believe that you did see that Myles character the following afternoon. However, I think that the man you saw was an actual person. He could have been someone you'd previously seen. Perhaps he was in the hotel reception when you checked in, and you only registered him in your subconscious. Then, when you fell asleep, your subconscious resurrected him and wove him into a dream. As for seeing him disappear through a locked door, well, are you sure you were close enough to be certain that was the door. Couldn't he have just gone into another room?'

Lydia considered what he'd said, and although she was sure she'd been correct about the door, Nick's theory made good sense. Yes, the more she thought about it, she had been exhausted when she'd arrived at the hotel yesterday and yes, the dream had been vivid and wonderful. Perhaps she was simply trying too hard to make it a reality, was it only wishful thinking? She began to question whether the man on the stairs had looked so much like Myles after all. She'd quite convinced herself it had all been an elaborate dream, when suddenly an image of Myles' vivid blue eyes burned into her memory; full of laughter and mischief... and something more. Her sudden intake of breath stopped them both in their tracks. 'What?' Nick said, searching her face.

'Whatever it was that I saw, I'm certain it wasn't a dream.' And handing Nick his jacket, she took up Billy's lead and walked purposefully home accompanied by the faint fragrance of honeysuckle hovering on the breeze.

Chapter Eight

Monday morning dawned and Lydia's diary was clear. Intending to make the most of her free day, she put Billy on his lead and made her way to the park. The good weather had drawn the crowds and so she walked through the park and up on to the moors.

Empty of livestock Billy was free to bounce along in the gorse and heather chasing butterflies. He splashed about in a natural pool to cool off then flopped down to doze in the shade. Lydia made her way to her favourite spot and settled down in a cluster of rocks to enjoy the rugged view. Breathing in the fresh clean air she began to relax. The sun was hot, and lulled by the gentle breeze and the buzzing of insects she leaned back against the rock and closed her eyes. The breeze caressed her arms, her cheeks. Something brushed her lips, her eyes flew open and she found she was gazing up at Myles Barringham.

'I'm sorry if I startled you, old bean. You fell asleep.'

Disorientated, Lydia looked around taking in the scene. She appeared to be in an orchard, sitting with her back against the base of a fruit tree. A huge surge of joy bubbled up. Wherever it was she'd been on Midsummer's Eve, she was back. Myles held out his hand and hauled her up.

His hand felt warm and dry, and he smelled of strawberries.

'Ready for a spot of tea, old bean? You completely missed the match you know.' He was dressed in cricket whites, a knife edge crease pressed into the flannels. 'Something up?' he said, when she didn't move.

'I'm not dressed appropriately,'

'Well now you come to mention it… Come on, there are some spares in the Ladies' hut. You might find a tennis dress or something that would suit.'

Inside, Lydia found a white dress. It reminded her of a sailor dress she'd worn as a child, with its low waist and square collar piped with navy blue. She quickly changed out of her jeans and T-shirt, but decided her white trainers would have to do. Myles was waiting when she emerged from the hut. He tucked her hand into the crook of his arm and they set off in the direction of the refreshment tent.

A waitress poured them chilled lemonade made from fresh lemons into tall sugar frosted glasses and popped a spring of mint on the top. The trestle table was groaning under the weight of food. Cucumber, and egg with cress sandwiches cut into triangles vied for space with dishes of strawberries topped with lashings of cream. A tiered cake-stand held pink and white fairy cakes and another was piled up high with scones surrounded by little pots of butter and jam and yet more cream. The waitresses looked hot and flustered in their uniform black dresses and stiffly starched white pinafore and bonnet. Very pre-French maid Lydia thought as one of them placed a silver teapot and hot water jug at their table. Myles didn't make to move, so Lydia poured the tea. Pre-women's lib as well, she realised, lifting the crocheted doily, which was covering the milk jug to keep the flies out. It was weighted down by pretty beads sewn around the edge. She made a mental note of the elaborate needlework before pouring milk into the cups.

Sipping the hot tea, she watched the milling crowd. The majority were merely spectators and she absorbed their fashion with a practiced eye. The food proved to be as delicious as it looked and she was quite disappointed to miss a second helping when Myles insisted on showing her the hall. 'Well my part of it anyway,' he said, walking to the front of the building.

Lydia recognised the façade: it was the building she'd stumbled upon after chasing Billy through the woods. The same building which had inexplicably been a ruin when she'd returned to it with her friends. It was now known as The Meadow Bank Hall Hotel. She knew for a fact that its interior was sleek and minimalist. Yet as she walked through the oak front door, the interior reverted once more to the Art Deco style she remembered from her dream, on the night of the

Midsummer's Eve Ball; only this time she knew she couldn't possibly be dreaming.

Myles began with a tour of his sitting room. They entered by the door she'd seen him walk through the day after the ball. The door which had been locked when she'd tried it, and which the member of staff had insisted belonged to an unoccupied room. Once inside, the furnishings took her breath away. The textiles, all stereotypical Art Deco, complimented the stunning examples of furniture and she recognised one or two rare pieces.

The bathroom, tiled in an abstract pattern of black and green, featured a roll top bath standing on claw feet. A huge chrome shower head was suspended over the bath, drooping like a giant sunflower sheltering its face from the rain. The linoleum floor was patterned in black and white squares, pristine and glossy. But it was the sight which greeted her as Myles opened the last door, which absurdly brought tears to her eyes. White muslin drapes billowed from the window and in front of that sunny place was a white crib, festooned with lace and muslin. Pale blue ribbons clasped the canopy. Crisp cotton curtains, with little blue rabbits and yellow chicks cheerfully contrasted with the snow-white muslin at the window. A large old bear eyed her sagely from his window seat, and a toy dog lay at the foot of the crib. Toy soldiers stood in rows, their bright red and black uniforms shiny and new, keeping guard in front of a most beautiful dolls' house. In one corner a large dapple grey rocking horse stood patiently waiting for a young rider. Dominating the room was a single bed covered by an exquisite quilt. It was made up of fabric alphabet blocks embroidered together. A bright and cheerful peg rug in blue, green and yellow covered the floor beside the bed. And a pair of tiny blue slippers with a train embroidered on each toe, waited strategically placed side by side for two tiny feet to jump into them. The room was enchanting. Engrossed, Lydia was suddenly aware Myles was watching her and she turned to look at him.

'This is traditionally the nursery wing,' he said, she raised a quizzical eyebrow.

'My godson sleeps here when he comes to visit. I've converted the suite of rooms for my personal use. Apart from the nursery itself, because it's so suited to the purpose and well, because my godson is a nice little chap and we have lots of fun when he comes to stay. Midnight feasts and the like. Well he thinks its midnight, it's usually more like eight o'clock.'

Myles strode across the room to open a large wooden toy chest. He lifted out a brightly painted wooden duck and placed it on the floor, then he raced around pulling it along behind him. The little creature paddled its feet as the wheels went around, flapping its wings and opening and closing its beak. 'Quack, quack!' shouted Myles. Lydia, thinking he was doing a good impression of the ducks outside the Fox and Duck, roared with laughter…

Instantly she was back on the moors, still laughing. Billy pounced on her, wanting to join in the fun. Her laughter dissolved into tears as reality dawned and she was forced to admit she'd been dreaming. She replayed the dream over and over in her mind and as the vivid images flooded her brain, her creative nature took over. She rummaged in the backpack for her sketchbook and pencils. In a frenzy, she began sketching, her pencil flying over the pages.

The sky was streaked red and gold by the time she and Billy walked down from the moors.

Next morning, she handed over the sketches to Jenny. 'What do you think?'

'These are amazing,' she said, flicking through excitedly. 'This is some of your best work, where did the inspiration come from?'

'Oh, just something I dreamed up,' she laughed, then the bell jingled announcing a customer.

Later that day, before the casual machinists went home, she called a meeting in the workroom. She passed around copies of the sketches and watched the women's reactions with pleasure.

'This is our new collection, and I intend to launch a huge publicity campaign to promote it. Of course, it's going to mean lots of over time if you're up for it.' She waited for the enthusiastic response to die down, then said, 'And how do you fancy getting paid double time for attending a party on the second Sunday of October, in the afternoon?'

'What's the catch?'

'You're only allowed one glass of Prosecco... Seriously though, I want you to model the new collection.'

'It'd take a whole bottle of Prosecco to get me on a catwalk.'

'That won't be necessary, we don't have room for a cat walk in the shop.'

'The party's going to be here?'

'Yes, 'An Afternoon of Fashion' with canapés and Champagne. I'll hire a catering company to serve the food and drinks, but rather than hire models, I want all of us to wear the new collection.' There were a few disgruntled mutterings, so Lydia said, 'Well, it was only a thought, I know most of you have family commitments at the weekends. Talk it over and let me know what you decide. There's no pressure, I just thought it might be a bit of fun to show off your hard work. You can keep the dress you wear and we'll design it to suit you especially. It's in all our interests to make you look gorgeous.'

'Why don't you just hire models? They'll have better figures than any of us.'

'You speak for yourself,' laughed a matronly member of staff, setting her double chins dancing.

'My idea is that we mingle with the customers, there's no-one more qualified to discuss our creations than the people who've created them. Most of our customers won't have model's figures either; they'll want to know how the clothes look on regular people. Anyway, that's all I wanted to say. I don't want to make you late leaving. Any questions or suggestions give me a shout. See you tomorrow.'

Lydia went through to the office and Pippa followed, 'Brilliant idea,' she said, 'and I just love the new sketches. I'm going to enjoy working with those fabrics. Shall we carry on with it tonight? I can make us a snack and go over the designs with you if you like?'

'Sounds like a plan,' Jenny said, coming into the office. She picked up the iPad and sat down on the opposite side of the desk. 'I'll start the 'to do' list. Fire away.'

'Make an appointment with the bank for a loan.' Lydia laughed.

'Next?'

'Place an advert in the paper and the local glossies. Then you'll need to contact the caterers, but don't let them supply the Champagne, I can get it wholesale. Oh, and book a Jazz band will you. Right Pippa, let's make a start on sorting out which fabrics we already have in stock and which need ordering.'

An advertisement appeared in the local glossy magazine in the form of a feature on Lydia and her shop. The newspapers ran an advertisement for three consecutive weeks, although all the tickets for the launch had gone by the end of the first. On the day of the event, Lydia was in the shop by six. She was peeling back the paper to reveal the window display just as an orange sun appeared on the horizon.

When she'd finished, she went outside to view the display from the street. The Edwardian façade and elegantly dressed square windows filled her with pride. The thrill of owning the shop had never faded. The window to the right of the door was a replica of the nursery room. She had incorporated a baby's christening gown and a selection of children's clothes. Satisfied everything was in place, she pressed the remote in her hand to activate the train set. The engine's whistle trilled loudly into the quiet morning every time it disappeared into the tunnel.

The second window, displayed an Art Deco sitting room. The pieces used in its creation were gathered from her personal collection or the internet. She pressed the remote to light the scene. A fire flickered invitingly in the hearth, but the lighting was too harsh. She pressed the dimmer and as the lights faded, an image of Lady

Barringham materialized in the armchair beside the fire. Her violet eyes fixed Lydia with a mischievous glint. Then she raised a glass of Champagne in salute before taking a sip and fading from view. Lydia ran inside the shop, it was empty. She searched the window, there was no one there.

Shaken, she went through to the workroom to make a coffee. Her mind in turmoil, she waited impatiently for the percolator to heat up and tried to think of a logical explanation. She was no nearer to finding one by the time the coffee was ready. She poured the hot liquid into a cup and carried it through to her office. There in the middle of the desk was a familiar guilt-edged envelope. The cup clattered from her hands before she'd taken a sip.

'Having a smashing time in here?' Jenny said, walking into the office. 'Do you know the front door's wide open...Lydia what's happened?'

'I don't know yet. I've just seen Lady Barringham sitting in the armchair in the window.'

'What, are you sure?'

'No, no I'm not sure, one minute she was there and the next she wasn't. Then I've just come in here and found that thing on the desk.'

Jenny retrieved the letter from the puddle of coffee and patted it dry with a paper tissue.

'Shall I open it?'

'Be my guest,'

Dear Miss Lockwood,

Further to our recent meeting, I wish to engage your services, with regards to a complete refurbishment throughout Barringham Hall. The design is to be a replica in style of those rooms which you viewed on your recent visits.

Please contact me directly at the hall, where we may finalise arrangements.

Looking forward to our next meeting.

Yours sincerely,

Myles Barringham

'What does he mean visits plural,' Jenny said, handing the letter to Lydia.

'Where do you think the ideas for the new collection came from? I'm afraid I can't take all the credit.'

'Sorry, you've lost me, what are you talking about.'

'Remember when you ask me where the inspiration came from, I told you it was something I'd dreamed up. Well I wasn't joking, that's exactly what happened, or at least I thought I must have been dreaming. Even when I saw Lady Barringham toasting me with Champagne I thought it was my imagination. You opened the letter. Am I dreaming now? You tell me, because I don't have a clue.'

'No, you're not dreaming, there has to be a logical explanation. Could she have got into the building while you were taking down the paper from the windows?

'She could have slipped past me while I was checking the windows from the street, the door was open.'

She took a fresh cup of steaming coffee from Jenny and sipped it gingerly. 'Thanks, that feels better already. You're right you know. Lady Barringham isn't a ghost. She's someone playing tricks, but I don't have time to figure out why just now. Come on we've a fashion launch to produce.'

Chapter Nine

'Well I think we deserve a celebration,' Jenny said, the morning after the launch, and began pouring a generous measure of brandy into everyone's cup of coffee. 'The response to our day of fashion has been phenomenal and we all played a part in that.'

'I took so many orders yesterday,' Pippa said, 'that I can guarantee full time hours for quite some time, if you're interested.'

'And,' Lydia added, 'if you can fulfil the extra orders at your usual production rate, I'll throw in a bonus,'

'We're in the money,' warbled two of the temporary workers, chinking their cups together.

'I'm not at all surprised that it was the nursery designs which stole the show,' Lydia said, 'but we've had so many orders through the website that we'll have to take on extra staff just for the packing.'

'My lad's looking for work.'

'Aye and my Dave's bored stiff since he retired. He's a good worker mind, just in case you were thinking he's past it.'

'Great, well tell them both to come in for a chat and we'll take it from there. Right now, I think we'd better make a start on those orders.'

They were so overwhelmed with work that it was towards the end of the following week before the subject of Myles Barringham came up again.

'Someone put that letter on your desk,' Jenny said, 'the question is who and why? What we need to do is find out if Barringham Hall actually exists, and if it does, we should be able to discover whether or not Myles and Lady Barringham exist.'

Their conversation was interrupted when Mrs. Cooper, their daily cleaner, poked her head around the door. 'All right if I do in here now dearies, is it? Only I've done everywhere else, and I'll miss my bus if I don't get a move on. The next one's not for another hour see, and I must get home in time to get my Dave's dinner, on account of him being on the night shift.'

They left her to it and went to do the cashing up.

'That's me on my way then,' Mrs Cooper said, half an hour later walking across the shop and buttoning up her coat. In the doorway, she stopped and turned, 'By the way dearies, I couldn't help overhearing your conversation earlier, about Barringham Hall. It does exist right enough. It's just that the locals always call it Meadow Bank Hall on account of its location. It's that new hotel, you know, the one where you went to that opening do, on Midsummer's Eve. Oh, I can see my bus coming, best dash, cheerio dearies,' and with a wave Mrs. Cooper left.

They watched her through the window, shuffling along not quite breaking into a trot with her feet at ten to two, clutching her shopping bag tightly to her ample bosom in hot pursuit of the bus.

'Well they always say if you want to know something ask the char lady,' Jenny laughed.

'I don't know whether I'm any the wiser or just confused by that revelation,' Lydia said, 'but I think it's time I paid our local Yank a call. I'd like to know if he can come up with an explanation for the mysterious Barringhams.'

'Aren't you worried he'll think you're bonkers?' Jenny said, frowning. 'It's a bit much to hit someone with at the first meeting.'

'Possibly, but I'll take along the sketches I drew after that dream tour of Myles apartment. If it goes badly, I can always pretend I'm touting for business.'

'The commission's for Barringham Hall, not the Meadow Bank Hall Hotel,' Jenny reminded her.

'I know what you're saying, but let's face it, if he doesn't know what we're talking about, then perhaps he should. If it's a hoax, it involves his business as well as ours.' She reached for the phone and keyed in the number, 'Good afternoon, my name's Lydia Lockwood of Deco Design. May I make an appointment to see the owner, Myles Barringham? Oh, really, my mistake. Grant Stevenson? I see. How long is he there for? No,

I'll contact you again, thank you for your help. Good bye,' Lydia disconnected the call. 'The owner's in America, and his name's Grant Stevenson. Whoever answered the phone didn't know anyone by the name of Barringham.'

The nights had drawn in and the weather turned cold. Billy slept contentedly in front of a roaring fire, while Lydia worked on refining her interior designs for Barringham Hall. Grant Stevenson was due back from America and she had an appointment to see him. Satisfied with her work, she turned on her laptop to check her e-mails. She delighted in zapping the spam, but her hand hovered over a genealogy website. Instead of deleting it, she followed the link and typed in the name Myles Barringham, Barringham Hall, Derbyshire. The search didn't find a match. She tried the name Barringham with Meadow Bank Hall, still no result, but the website recommended searching Parish records. She left the genealogy site and searched Grant Stevenson. The search brought up his US and UK websites and the recent press releases on The Meadow Bank Hall Hotel, but she couldn't find any previous connection between Grant Stevenson and the building. She logged out and reached for her mobile, 'Hi Jenny,' she said, 'How do you fancy making a weekend of our trip to see Grant Stevenson? There's something I want to check out before the meeting.'

Chapter Ten

After morning service, Lydia approached the Reverend Byewaters with her request to look in the Parish records. 'Good morning to you,' he said, shaking her hand. 'As it happens I'm rather interested in genealogy myself. The records are kept in the Vestry. I'm just on my way there, if you'd care to join me? With luck my housekeeper should have left a fresh pot of tea.' They followed him along a dark musty corridor and into a room flooded with sunlight. 'Ah, here we are!' he said, opening the glass doors of a large bookcase and lifting down a leather-bound volume. He placed it on the table and leafed through the pages until he found what he was looking for. 'The marriage of Augustus Charles Barringham to Clarissa Elizabeth Brookes, the 26th December 1889,' he read aloud, before turning the ledger so Lydia and Jenny could read it. Then he took a delicate sip of his tea and leaned back in his chair, munching on a digestive biscuit. 'The christenings in those days followed quite quickly after the marriages so you can use the marriage dates as a bench mark to guide you. I wonder if I could leave you to browse while I work on my evening sermon,' he said.

Jenny found the christening record for the Barringham's first born, a son Frederick William, and then a daughter Sophia Elizabeth, who was christened just over a year later. The final entry for the family was another boy, Myles Edward Barringham.

'So, now you know,' Jenny said, 'a Myles Barringham did once exist, but how does that change anything?'

'I'm not sure, not yet anyway. I just needed to know.'

'Look here,' Jenny said, pointing to an entry in the register of deaths. Sophia died before her first birthday,'

'Oh, that's so sad,'

'And look at this entry, Frederick was killed during World War One. There doesn't seem to be an entry for Myles or his parents. So perhaps they didn't die in this parish.'

They found the Reverend at his desk in an anti-room just off the vestry. 'Well now,' he said, after hearing what they'd discovered. 'I'm obviously not old enough to have remembered the Barringham family personally, but I do know that the hall fell into disrepair and was closed up during the late Nineteen-Twenties. I believe Lord and Lady Barringham went to live with relatives. Of course, their eldest son was killed in action in France. The younger son seems to have been something of the black sheep. Rumour has it that he absconded with the family jewels intended to fund the upkeep of the hall. They must have been worth a considerable fortune if indeed that were the case. Well I'm afraid I must lock up now. If any further information concerning the Barringham's comes to light, I will gladly contact you.'

'Thank you,' Lydia said, handing him her business card.

'I see you're a designer. Then you will appreciate more than most, what a great pity it is, that such a beautiful building has been so violated over the years. Yet another loss to our English heritage,' he sighed, shaking his head. 'Still,' he brightened, 'at least one should be grateful that it is now a hotel and not a ruin. I did hear that a young American has taken it over with a view to returning it to its former glory, though of course it will still be a hotel.'

'Yes, I heard that too,' Lydia replied. Then shaking his hand and thanking him for his help, Lydia and Jenny left him to lock up.

That evening after dinner, they wandered through the hotel and into the flagged courtyard at the centre of the building. The original three tier fountain was bubbling away cascading down into a large stone basin. The weather had turned remarkably mild for the time of year and Jenny suggested they sit on the bench resting against the mellow sandstone wall. It was pleasant sitting in companionable silence listening to the trickle of water. A golden moon hovered in an ink blue sky and the air was thick with the scent of honeysuckle. Lydia closed her eyes and breathed in the heavenly scent. 'How wonderful it must have been to be a part of the privileged classes between wars,' she sighed. 'Imagine walking and riding for hours across your own land or driving down country lanes free from traffic congestion.'

'Imagine having a wardrobe full of divine clothes to wear,' Jenny yawned sleepily.

'You've got those now,' Lydia laughed.

'Yes, but I don't have a house full of servants organising them.'

'It's neither as idyllic nor as simple as that,' a familiar voice whispered. Lydia's eyes snapped open and she saw Myles standing there. He was glaring at her with such intensity she was taken aback, more by his expression than his sudden appearance. There wasn't a glimmer of the usual mischief evident in his eyes tonight.

'Remember, Lydia, I tried. Whatever you may hear about me, always remember that I did the best I could under the circumstances to do my duty. Try to save Barringham Hall where I have failed.' He lifted her hand and kissed the tips of her fingers before turning and striding out of the courtyard. As she watched his retreating figure, his apparition along with the heady scent of honeysuckle evaporated. Looking around, she saw that everything was the same as it had been moments earlier.

Jenny stretched her arms above her head and sighed contentedly. 'Did you ever see such a magical sky?'

'Didn't you see him?'

'See who,'

'Myles, just now.'

'No, I was busy looking at the moon,' she sighed.

'Didn't you hear him talking to me?'

'What, you think Myles was here,' Jenny said, beginning to concentrate on what Lydia was saying. 'There's only been the two of us sitting here for the last twenty minutes.'

Lydia began to shiver. Myles had seemed what... hopeless, demoralized? Something had changed, something important. This was different to all their previous meetings. Why, she wondered, if he was a figment of her imagination, would she dream up a depressed Myles when she much preferred the happy carefree version? She searched for a clue in his words. He said he'd tried. What was it he had tried to do? Clearly, he had asked her to trust him. She had no idea with what.

'Lydia, are you alright?' Jenny asked studying her face.

'Yes, yes I'm good. Can you smell honeysuckle?'

'I could earlier, but I don't know where it was coming from. It's too late in the year. Look over there,' she said, pointing to the woody branches of a honeysuckle trained against the wall, 'that plant's been cut back.'

Strangely, Lydia no longer felt afraid, only curious. She was looking forward to the meeting with Grant Stevenson tomorrow.

Promptly at nine o'clock next morning, Lydia handed her business card over to the receptionist.

'Ah, Miss Lockwood, we've been trying to contact you on your mobile. I'm afraid the flight that Mr. Stevenson is on has had to make an unscheduled stop over. He's unsure when he'll arrive back in England. I'm so sorry, but you'll have to make an alternative appointment. If you wouldn't mind waiting, I'll ask his secretary to come down to see you. It's a little more private over there,' she said, indicating a cluster of bucket chairs grouped around a low table. 'Can I offer you a complimentary pot of tea or coffee?'

'We're fine thank you,' Lydia said, making for the chairs.

'Do you think she's telling the truth?' Jenny said, sitting down beside her.

'Don't know yet, I'll check my phone for missed calls. Yes, she's right, two calls last night and one this morning. The sound's, turned off. I must have forgotten to switch it back on after the church service yesterday. I suppose it serves me right for booking in under your name, and not mentioning our appointment, otherwise they'd have left a message on the room answer phone.'

'I meant was she telling the truth about his flight being delayed, or do you think he's avoiding us?'

'Only time will tell on that one.' As she looked up, Lydia saw Myles standing at the foot of the stairs, holding a flight bag in one hand and a suit carrier in the other. He was smiling at the receptionist, and he had never looked more handsome. Surprisingly he was wearing denims and a white shirt, a snug fit over his muscular frame. The white linen enhanced his golden tan and the sun had streaked his hair. His blue eyes sparkled like crystals even at this distance. She clasped Jenny's wrist, 'It's ok,' Jenny winced. 'I see him too.' Mesmerized they watched as he mounted the stairs.

'Come on,' Lydia said, and dragged Jenny after her. They reached the top of the stairs in time to see him enter the door to the private wing. Lydia let go of Jenny's wrist and ran along the corridor. She flung herself against the door and hammered loudly. Hot on her heels, Jenny tried to peel her away. 'What the hell do you think you're doing?' she said, 'You'll get us thrown out!'

With determined effort, Lydia broke free and launched herself at the door again. This time it gave way and she hurtled into the room.

He was standing next to the fireplace. The room was rather dingy by comparison to the rest of the hotel, but sunlight from a floor to ceiling bay window flooded one half of it. On closer inspection, she could see that the man's features were rugged and more irregular than Myles, but the similarity was startling and the eyes were identical, although this man's eyes reflected mistrust more than mischief.

'Who are you?' she said.

'Pardon me Ma'am, but I'm thinking that should be my line, since you happen to be in my apartment.'

It was then that she noticed the portrait, still partly encased in its packaging. It was perched precariously on the mantel piece. She brushed past him and began peeling back the remaining brown paper.

'Just what the hell do you think you're doing?' he said.

She didn't answer. She was transfixed, her face illuminated by the fire's glow had taken on an angelic quality. 'Who is he?' she whispered.

'Myles Barringham, my great-grandfather.' He tried to catch her as her knees buckled, but she was out cold before she hit the floor.

Chapter Eleven

Pippa was alone in the shop. It had been an unusually quiet day. She was busy sorting through the paper work when she uncovered the veterinary brochure. Seeing Nick James face smiling up at her from the front cover twisted her stomach into a jealous knot.

'Gosh, you're gorgeous,' she said to his image. Jealousy wasn't an emotion Pippa was familiar with, but the green-eyed monster had its claws firmly embedded as far as Nick and Lydia were concerned. She was finding it more difficult as time went on to conceal her emotions, particularly as Nick had taken to calling into the shop most afternoons on his way to evening surgery. His visits always seemed to coincide with Lydia's absence and that's how Pippa had got to know him, and unfortunately for her, fallen in love with him. She lived for his visits, but they were bitter sweet.

'Give me half a chance,' she said now, to his smiling image, 'but you're not interested in me, are you?' He had never been anything other than friendly. In the beginning, when he first began calling while she was alone in the shop, she had tried to read his body language. She'd looked for a sign, a gleam in his eye, or anything which might give her hope, but she had come up with zilch, not so much as a flicker. 'That's the last time I'll bother making a wish on a shooting star,' she sighed, putting the brochure back in the drawer.

Outside there was a screech of tyres, a sickening crunch of metal and shattering glass. A car horn blared incessantly, and then the shop door crashed open with such force it slammed itself shut again, leaving Nick James standing there. She thought for a moment she'd conjured him up.

'There's been an accident,' he shouted, bringing her to her senses. 'I'll need towels and bandages. Do you have a first aid kit?'

Spurred into action she gave him the kit and then ran upstairs to get towels from Lydia's flat. She then found some suitable material to tear into bandages. Picking up a spare first aid bag she ran into the street after Nick, locking the shop door as she went. She soon assessed the situation and launched into action. Her training taking over.

'Has anyone called an ambulance?'

'On its way,' shouted a bystander. She ran over to the car which had crashed into a lamp post. The woman driver slumped over the wheel had a nasty gash on her head which was bleeding profusely. The airbag hadn't deployed. Pippa didn't want to move her for fear of spinal injury, but set about dressing the wound. She breathed a sigh of relief when she heard the sirens.

Leaving the paramedics to do their job, she ran over to where Nick was kneeling beside a rough haired collie, pressing a towel against a gaping hole in the dog's leg. Its white paws and bib were soaked in blood. 'Lassie,' she whispered, and was rewarded with a flicker of a smile from Nick.

'How can I help?' she asked.

'We need to get him out of the road, he's lost a lot of blood. Here, my car keys are in this left pocket, if you can lay the seat flat I can ride in the back with him. Can you drive us to the surgery?'

Pippa moved with the speed of an Olympic sprinter and together they managed to get the unconscious animal into the car. Then, driving as fast as possible, she set off towards the surgery.

The beautiful Collie looked lifeless on the operating table. 'Can you phone Helen my practice nurse?' You'll find her number in my mobile. Explain what's happened and ask her to come in to give me a hand. It's her day off, but she'll not mind when she knows what's up.'

After a brief conversation, she switched off the mobile. 'Helen's at the coast, she won't make it back in time.'

'Bloody hell, of course she is. I'd forgotten about that in all the excitement. Well I'll have to manage without her or this boy won't make it.'

'I'll help,' she said, reaching for a cap and gown.

'Oh, no you won't. I've enough to cope with here, without you passing out on me and knocking instruments all over the place.'

'Two year's nurses training any good?'

A flicker of amusement reached his eyes. 'Scrub away,' he said, then he turned his back on her to prepare the animal for surgery.

Chapter Twelve

Lydia woke to discover she was lying on a huge four poster bed with Jenny on one side and a stranger checking her pulse on the other. 'Welcome back young lady, Morrison's the name, I'm the hotel doctor. How are you feeling?'

'Embarrassed!'

He asked her a few more questions and after checking her blood pressure, prescribed nothing more than a cup of tea. 'You can bring that tea in now,' he called through to the sitting room. The Myles clone appeared almost at once carrying a tray. Lydia looked from the doctor's kind grey eyes into his clear blue ones, now twinkling at her in a most familiar way.

'Grant Stevenson,' he said, placing the tray beside the bed. 'It's not every day an attractive woman bursts into my apartment and drops at my feet. Do you have an explanation or is this something you do on a regular basis?'

Colour flooded her cheeks, how could she explain her reaction to the portrait without him thinking a deranged woman had stormed his apartment.

Fortunately for her, Jenny took control. 'Mr Stevenson,' she said, 'we owe you an explanation as well as an apology. This is Lydia Lockwood and I'm Jennifer Thompson, our company is Deco Design. We were told that our appointment with you this morning had been cancelled because your plane was delayed. We were waiting to speak to your secretary, when Lydia mistook you for someone else.'

'Mistaken identity is not unusual, I can accept that, but what's with the dramatic entrance and the fainting act in front of the portrait?'

'Hardly an act, Mr. Stevenson, but I'll come to that in a moment. Someone claiming to be the owner of this hotel has commissioned us to refurbish it. We aren't sure whether that person is genuine or a hoaxer.'

'Too damn right they're a hoaxer. I haven't commissioned any refurbishment.'

He was leaning, half sitting against a walnut desk, both hands resting on the leather top. Jenny could feel the arrogance oozing out of him. She studied his face, he thinks I'm shooting him a line, she thought, and felt an overwhelming urge to shock the smugness from him.

'Mr. Stevenson, please understand that we are telling you the truth. We're every bit as puzzled by recent events as I'm sure you are right now. We simply wanted to inform you that someone appears to be targeting our business and linking it directly to this hotel.'

Lydia returned the cup and saucer to the tray and came to stand beside Jenny. 'Several months ago, I served a woman calling herself Lady Barringham. The woman was dressed entirely in Twenties style, even down to the make-up and hair style. I just passed her off as being a bit eccentric. You see most of our vintage designs are bought for special occasions, not regular wear. When the cheque she'd paid with turned out to be a pre-World War II bank draft, I realised she must be some sort of a hoaxer. She never did return for the dress, and she cost us a lot of time, working on the alterations.'

'Here, see for yourself,' Jenny said, fumbling in her file for the bank draft, 'the bank returned it.'

Some of his arrogance dissolved and Lydia, determined to find out if he knew more than he was letting on, said, 'The woman was dressed in lemon crepe de chine with a matching cloche hat. She had jet black hair, cut in a bob and her eyes were an unusual violet colour. Do you know a woman who looks like that Mr. Stevenson?'

He half turned his head, as though about to look over his shoulder but changed his mind, Lydia couldn't see what had drawn his attention.

'This building is known locally as Meadow Bank Hall. We've discovered it's actually Barringham Hall, but I expect you already know that,' Jenny said, handing him the guilt-edged envelope with the sealing wax crest still intact. 'Do you recognise that Coat of Arms? Look at the address on the letter inside and at the signature.' Jenny delighted in seeing the last trace of smugness drain from his face as he studied the letter. 'See how short the telephone number is,' she pointed out. 'It would be interesting to discover, whether that's the original number for Barringham Hall. Here's the calling card that accompanied the bank draft. The contact details match those on the letter.'

'I've brought along some sketches to show you,' Lydia said, retrieving the file from Jenny.

The cynical look was back on his face. She could almost hear him thinking, ah now we're getting to the point, I knew you had an angle somewhere. His expression slipped again after he'd given the sketches a cursory glance.

'Where did you get these designs from?' his tone was accusing.

'I told you I sketched them.'

'Where did you find the designs to sketch them,' he responded sarcastically.

'You wouldn't believe me if I told you.'

'Try me.'

'Very well, on the opening night of the hotel, I was supposed to be attending the ball, but I fell asleep in my hotel room. In a dream, I met a man the image of your great-grandfather and we spent the evening together at a house party. We were here in this building, but it looked entirely different. I sketched what I saw in the dream, it's as simple as that.'

'You're right,' he said, 'I don't believe you. Come over here, I want to show you something.' He opened the desk drawer and pulled out a sheaf of bound documents. He untied the ribbon and spread them out on the desk. 'These were recently found in my grandfather's house in America. They're virtually identical to your sketches. Now tell me where did you copy those designs from?'

'I'm telling you the truth.'

'Do you expect me to believe that?'

'No I don't actually. Any more than I can believe I was dreaming when I was wandering through this building in the Nineteen-Twenties cavorting about with your great-grandfather, playing party games and dancing on the terrace in the moonlight. But to admit to anything else, would be to admit that I'm probably quite mad, and I can assure you that I am not. I told you, I sketched what I saw. I don't have any other explanation. Here's my business card. If you want to discuss it further, then you can reach me on any of those numbers.'

Grant Stevenson stood at his window and watched Lydia's car cruise down the drive and out of sight. A lazy smile graced his lips, all signs of jet lag had disappeared. 'Lydia Lockwood,' he said, 'what an intriguing woman you are.'

He walked over to his desk and lifted out a package from behind it. It was the other portrait of the pair of portraits found in his grandfather's attic. A shiver ran along his spine as he peeled away the brown paper, he knew the painting was of the young woman who Lydia Lockwood had described as Lady Barringham. Grant looked at the newly restored brass plaque… Lady Lydia Fay Barringham c1922.

Chapter Thirteen

The operation on the dog had gone well. Pippa's stomach had churned alarmingly and the familiar buzzing had started in her ears, but she'd managed to stay on her feet. Sheer determination keeping her going. Thankfully Nick was too busy with the patient to notice her inner struggle. He hadn't saved the leg but he'd saved the dog.

The waiting room was full by the time the operation was over and Nick launched straight into evening surgery. Pippa knew he would stay with the dog that night, or at least until it had recovered from the anaesthetic. Here was the chance she'd been waiting for. If the way to a man's heart is through his stomach, she thought, then I'm about to play my trump card.

Her timing was perfect. She floated through the doorway in an aromatic cloud, just as Nick was seeing the last patient out.

'Thought you might be hungry,' she said, seeing his puzzled frown. 'Where's your kitchen.'

She put her packages on the worktop and took out a table cloth, she gave it a practiced flick and it unfolded mid- air to descended like a parachute over the table.

'Corkscrew and two glasses please,' she said, handing him a bottle of wine before placing the steaming casserole in the centre of the table.

She lifted the lid to allow the meaty aroma to circulate and cut open a crusty loaf, fresh from the oven. 'Don't just stand there, that dog will be awake soon and then no doubt you'll let your dinner go cold.'

'I can't believe you've gone to so much trouble,' he said, scooping a large forkful of succulent steak into his mouth. 'It's really good of you, this is absolutely delicious!'

Pippa felt the warm glow of success. Just you wait until you've tasted my strawberry shortcake, she thought.

The dog was taking longer to recover than anticipated. Nick had checked the animal over several times but couldn't find anything wrong. He decided to leave it to sleep a while longer. He was about to climb the stairs up to his apartment when the surgery phone rang. The conversation was brief.

'Good news,' he said, entering the living room. 'That was the dog's owner on the phone. The police gave them the number. They'll be along in the morning.'

'How's he doing?'

'Still out, it's probably the shock to his system as much as anything. A good long sleep is what he needs right now. Shall I open another bottle of wine? Or would you prefer coffee?'

'It's getting late, I'd better be going home, I'll just rinse through the dishes I brought.'

'Leave them,' he said. 'I'll do it. I can bring them over tomorrow. Come on, I'll walk you home. He reached for her coat and helped her on with it. She turned to thank him.

'It's me who should be thanking you,' he said, adjusting her collar. 'You saved that animal's life today.' She began to protest but he interrupted. 'No, I'd have given it my best shot, but in hindsight, if I'd operated alone, I'd have lost him. You're a natural you know. Why did you quit nursing?'

'No choice really, kept passing out in the operating theatre.' It took Nick a moment or two to realise the implication behind what she'd just said, then he roared with laughter.

'Oh, be quiet, you'll disturb the dog,' she said, pressing her fingertips to his lips. He clasped her hand and turned it over, his thumb stroking her wrist as he planted a kiss in the palm. She quivered at his touch and a fire ignited deep inside as his kisses captured her lips. His mouth was skilful and probing, leaving her lips throbbing with longing as he rained kisses her over cheeks, her eyes, her throat. Her needy response fuelled his desire, and she clung to him her senses reeling. Never once, in all the hours spent daydreaming about him, had she imagined such ecstasy from one kiss.

Nick lifted his head, 'Have you any idea how long I've waited to do that,' he said.

'But what about all the time you've spent at the shop waiting to see Lydia?'

'Plucking up the courage to ask you out. Did you never wonder how I always managed to miss her quite so spectacularly?'

'You have got to be kidding me.'

'Quiet. You'll wake the dog,' he said, tugging at her lower lip, and smothering her laughter with kisses.

They walked arm in arm along the deserted streets. The damp night was pungent with fallen leaves and wood smoke. Pippa looked up at the single star, hanging beside a crescent moon, like a solitaire in the black sky. Perhaps it was too soon to believe her wish was coming true.

At her front door, Nick said, 'See you tomorrow?'

'Yes, at the surgery. I'll bring a picnic. If we can't leave our patient, we can eat it in the surgery. Although if everything's going well, how about taking a boat out on the river?'

'In this weather?'

'I'll bring rugs and hot soup.'

'Are you always this assertive?'

'Only when it matters,' she said, standing on tiptoe to kiss the tip of his nose. Then she turned and went inside.

Nick stared at the closed door. He hoped he mattered very much to this intelligent, witty, beautiful girl.

Chapter Fourteen

Although Grant was exhausted, it was a fitful sleep. Images of Lydia Lockwood kept mingling with the portrait images of Lydia Barringham. And images of the plantation house kept getting mixed up with those of the derelict Barringham Hall. His great-grandparents met him at the entrance, as they had in the previous dream, only this time the old building was newly refurbished as the hotel, in its current minimalist state. Yet once again when they led him through the building each room transformed into the Art Deco style. Inexplicably, he found himself back at the hotel entrance. Lydia Lockwood was running up the steps. She ran straight into his open arms and he held her tightly, she smelled of honeysuckle. The dream slipped away on a sigh and he fell into a deep contented sleep.

It was dark when Grant woke and for a moment he couldn't think where he was. He reached for his phone to check the time, it said 19:25PM. Drowsy from the effects of jet lag, he staggered into the shower and let the fierce spray of hot water ease his stiff limbs. It had been a month of shocks and surprises for Grant, starting with the death of his beloved Gramps. Even on the flight home for the funeral, he'd been unable to comprehend that the cheerful man with the greying hair, and twinkling blue eyes the image of his own, would not be waiting for him at the airport. Gramps had been his confidant, his mentor and his inspiration.

He quickly dressed and headed for the dining room. His intention was to observe the type of clientele the hotel was attracting, but once the smell of food reached him, he realised he was ravenously hungry. He ordered steak and chips and a bottle of house red. It was very disappointing. He marvelled that people bothered to dine there at all. He pushed his plate aside making a mental note to check out their suppliers before speaking to the chef. He sat back pretending to drink the truly revolting wine while observing the other diners. Were they stereotypical, or a diverse example? He spotted the business types instantly, recognising in them a kindred spirit.

Looking to the far side of the dining room, he saw both young and elderly couples dining in a more secluded, romantic corner of the room. A candle's flame, flickered in the breeze, as one couple stepped onto the terrace. What were they celebrating? He could see them clearly through the large widows and the sight of them in the moonlight, sharing an intimate moment, stirred in him an emotion he couldn't at first fathom. Realisation when it came was uncomfortable…it was envy.

The couple stepped back inside and the girl, admiring the solitaire on her finger, twisted her hand this way and that to catch the light as she made her way to their table. A bottle of Champagne was waiting on ice. An image of his great-grandparents looking glamorous in the portraits flashed into his head. Theirs was a romantic story. They had eloped and sailed to America. He wondered if they'd truly been as happy as his family believed them to be. They'd certainly made a success of their lives.

He wasn't in the mood for socializing, so he returned to his room. After pouring himself a brandy, he went to sit by the fire in his favourite comfortable, shabby leather chair. Staring into the flames his thoughts turned to Lydia Lockwood. How indignant she'd looked bursting into his rooms, like a fiery angel. Her breasts had heaved so alarmingly; he'd felt in danger of being shot by a shirt button. He steered his thoughts away from Lydia's heaving breasts and all at once the jet lag caught up with him again. Putting the brandy aside he crawled into bed. It was not to be the peaceful slumber he'd hoped for. He was troubled by another of the dreams which had plagued him since finding the portraits...

The fair haired young man in Military Uniform sat writing at a leather topped desk in the bay window of a book lined study. A door opened and a pretty young woman entered the room. She was the epitome of an Edwardian maid, covered from neck to toe in a black dress, its severity relieved only by a white starched apron and bonnet. Instantly the soldier was on his feet and in two strides he'd crossed the room. Gathering her in his arms, he kissed her hungrily. Wriggling free, she ran over to the fireplace, tucking her raven curls under the bonnet as she went. Her cheeks were flushed, but her violet eyes sparkled with love. 'Now Sir,' she said, 'that's no way for a gentleman to behave with the lady's maid, even if she does happen to be covering for the house maid.' He chuckled, a deep husky sound and made a grab for her, but she ducked under his arm. 'I am here, Sir, to light your fire.'

At that, he roared with laughter. 'I'm always on fire when you're in the room, Polly.'

'Shhh! The Mistress will hear, and she'll want to know what you're laughing at.'

'Dash it all Polly! Can't a fellow laugh in his own study without permission?'

'Certainly Sir, but not in front of the servants.'

His laughter drained away and he looked stricken. 'That won't be the case for much longer Polly, you'll see. That's the one good thing to come out of the carnage of this damned insufferable war. More rights for the working man, and woman too, for that matter. The trade unions are becoming powerful, Polly. And the women, well they're proving they can manage a man's work equally well. Servants are learning they can earn twice as much in industry, as working for the likes of me and mine. The social gap is narrowing; you mark my words Polly.'

'Get away with you. You'll be saying women'll have the vote next,' she scoffed.

In two strides, he'd narrowed the gap between them, and taking her in his arms he crushed her to him. 'Polly,' he whispered, nibbling her ear. 'When I leave for my billet at the end of the week, come with me. My battalion is to be stationed near the coast for a further week before we sail for France.'

Her violet eyes widened in horror and she tried to squirm free, but he held her fast.

'Please don't ask that of me,' she said, 'you know I would do anything for you, but I won't soil my reputation and lose my job for the sake of one week together.'

The young man's face looked grief stricken until realisation dawned, 'Polly, my dearest, darling girl. My sincere apologies for what must count as the clumsiest of proposals. I'm asking you to be my wife. We can get a special license and honeymoon together for a few days at least. Oh, Polly, please say you will. Once we're married, we can live anywhere we choose, with or without our families blessing. I can obtain a commission after the war is over. We might not be rich, but it will bring in a bob or two, and I believe an Officer's family quarters are rather top notch.'

She seemed stunned into silence, though it took only a moment to reach her decision.

Screaming at the top of her voice, she threw her arms around his neck, showering him in kisses.

The door swung open and in the doorway, her back ramrod straight, stood a woman wearing a dress the colour of steel. Her hair was greying at the temples and coiled about her head, secured by decorative pins. 'I heard a scream,' she said, squinting through pincer spectacles perched on the bridge of her nose. 'What exactly is going on here?'

'Hello Mother,' the young man said cheerfully enough, releasing the maid from his grasp. 'Polly was laying the fire and I'm afraid a mouse ran out of the kindling and gave her rather a fright.'

A horrified gasp escaped the older woman, 'Good heavens, where is it now?' she said, gathering her skirts tightly about her legs. 'Don't stand there, snivelling girl, go and find Barraclough. Tell him to come at once, no matter what he is attending to!'

The maid dipped a curtsey and made her escape, running like the wind along the corridor. Once on the back stairs, her laughter exploded and she doubled up trying to quell her joy. 'As long as I live,' she told the deserted staircase, 'I'll never forget the look on her hoity-toity face... *What are you doing with my son?*' she mimicked, hands on her hips flouncing down the stairs. 'That's what you were really thinking, you old shrew. Even if you didn't say it.' She cast her eyes upwards. Then as though a sudden thought had occurred, she sat down heavily on the stone step. 'One day the young master will be a Lord... Crickey!' she said, getting to her feet and walking on down the stairs, 'That'll make me a Lady.'

'Aye, Lady Muck,' the cook said to her, as she stepped into the kitchen. 'What have you been doing upstairs until now? There's ten pounds of spuds waiting to be peeled.' Pulling herself up to her full height, the maid looked the cook straight in the eye and said, 'If you will excuse me for a moment longer, I have a very important message for Mr Barraclough.' Then with her nose in the air and as much grace as she could muster, she sauntered over to where Barraclough was polishing silver in the scullery.

Grant woke lathered in sweat, his thoughts in a jumble. He'd thrashed his covers onto the floor, the room was stifling. He stumbled over to the mini bar and downed a bottle of ice cold water, then wrapping his nakedness in a sheet, he opened the French doors and stepped onto the balcony. An orange sun was rising on the horizon, its glow shrouded in mist. He greedily gulped in great lungsful of crisp air.

Gazing over the gardens, he felt that nothing had been quite the same since he'd bought this building. That wasn't strictly true of course and he acknowledged subtle changes had been happening ever since he'd discovered the portraits. He wondered what his great-grandfather would have made of this latest acquisition. Myles had been the first in the family to recognise the value of acquiring real estate and converting a building's purpose, to meet demand. He'd arrived in America as a penniless newlywed except for his wife's jewels. Before his life was over, Myles had developed several dockside premises, a hotel complex with a cabaret restaurant and casino rooms, and made a home for his family out of the plantation house. He'd employed many people and his greatest achievement, in Grant's opinion, was that he'd managed to bring his employees and his businesses safely through the Wall Street crash.

Grant wished Gramps was here to talk things over with. The eerie call of a single bird echoed in the distance. He felt very alone.

Chapter Fifteen

'What you need,' declared Jenny, shattering the silence in the car, 'is a holiday.' Lydia continued to stare at the road ahead. She was feeling emotionally drained and quite ridiculous. Maybe she had spent too many years looking to the past. Then she remembered what the Twenties had been all about, innovative and vibrant young people, full of energy living in the moment seeking out daring adventures.

Jenny felt the shift in her mood, 'Feeling better now?' she said, squeezing her hand.

'You're right you know, I could do with a holiday, I'll give mum and dad a call.'

Lydia saw her father waiting eagerly at arrivals. His crinkly face already beaming in anticipation. She missed both her parents terribly since they emigrated, but father and daughter had a special bond. Suddenly she was overwhelmed with a longing to hug him and she ran to close the distance separating them. She took him by surprise, momentarily knocking him off balance as she launched herself at him. It was the first time she had noticed signs of his advancing years.

'Whoa there, pumpkin, steady on. You nearly had me over.' He held her away from him to look at her beaming face. 'My, aren't you the sight for sore eyes,' he laughed.

'Oh, dad, I've missed you so much. I've been so busy with work; I didn't realise how much until just now. Where's mum? I thought she'd be here to meet me.'

'She's driving around. There was nowhere to park and I was worried that you'd arrive with no-one to greet you.'

'Ever the thoughtful one,' she said, kissing his cheek. Then with her arms linked through his, they walked out of the airport in search of her mother.

'You look worn out, poor darling.'

'Nice to see you too, mum,' Lydia replied, kissing her mother's cheek before scrambling into the back of the car.

'Well you've come to the right place for some peace and relaxation,' her mother said, driving out of the airport heading in the direction of home.

Lydia sat with one foot dangling in the pool, sipping an ice cold Spritza, looking out to the horizon. She had been at the villa just over a week, and her parents and their beautiful home had worked their magic. Her skin had developed a light, sun kissed glow, and the tight band of pain around her head had eased until it had completely disappeared. She woke refreshed each morning from a dreamless sleep and Myles and the worrying images had faded into the realms of fantasy. Standing up, she slipped out of her silk robe and dived into the pool. She swam two lengths and surfaced to find her father standing at the edge. 'John's on the phone,' he said, 'he wants to know if we'll join him for a drink at the Beach Bar. Would you like to come, or would you prefer some time to yourself?'

'I'd love to come. I remember John and Claudia from my last visit, they're an entertaining couple.'

'Eccentric more like,' he chuckled. 'Ok I'll let him know you're joining us.'

The night was sultry even for the Canaries. White lights twinkled in the trees lining the promenade and giant palms swayed in the slight breeze coming off the ocean. The globe street lights reminded Lydia of the harvest moon she and Jenny had sat under, the night they'd stayed at The Meadow Bank Hall Hotel. It was the last time she'd seen Myles. She furtively looked at the innocent crescent moon hovering overhead and quickened her pace to catch up with her parents.

Her mood lifted the moment she stepped into the vibrant bar. She was immediately surrounded by waiters admonishing her for staying away so long. The bar was open to the elements on three sides and colourful lights twinkled from the eaves. Red and white checked cloths covered the tables, and candles stuffed into bottles flickered merrily, almost in rhythm with the seventies music, coming from an ancient stereo system behind the bar. A bohemian mix of musicians, artists and other theatrical souls gathered at the Beach Bar to eat and drink, be creative and merry.

Down on the beach a huge bonfire flickered. Its red and yellow flames illuminating a gathering of people dotted about the sand. Several were strumming guitars while others grilled sausages and baked potatoes by the heat of the fire. Lydia was drawn almost hypnotically down the steps and on towards the fire. Someone called to her to join them and someone else put a bottle in her hand. Suddenly she was a part of this happy gathering. Incense sticks burned in the sand filling the air with their heady scent. Both men and women wore plaited braids around their heads and wrists. Their hair tumbled wild and curly over their shoulders. Beads and bells adorned tie dyed kaftans and shirts, and elaborate waistcoats studded with tiny mirrors woven into the fabric, reflected the firelight. She thought for one wild moment, that she'd travelled back in time to the Seventies, but then she saw her parents standing on the balcony watching her. They raised their glasses, then turned to speak to John and Claudia.

The surf pounded the beach incessantly. Each wave rearing up like an angry sea dragon poised to pounce, before spewing foam, bubbling and frothing over the sand. Glittering turquoise phosphorescent shimmered brightly against the black of the ocean as it caught glimpses of moonlight.

'Magical, isn't it?' Lydia said, to the girl sitting beside her.

'Yeah, awesome,' came the response and Lydia felt tempted to add, 'Yeah cool man,' until speech temporarily deserted her when several people ran naked into the glittering foam. One guy, thankfully wearing shorts, broke away from the group and hauled her up off the sand. Holding her hand, he pulled her laughing and fully clothed, straight into the ocean. She dived cutting through the arc of a wave, and another, before spinning around onto her back and giving herself up to the motion of the water. Someone called out, and momentarily distracted, she caught a wave full on and was plunged deep into the centre of the frothing white surf. Thrashing about and unable to stand on the sliding shingle, she was floundering until two strong arms hoisted her up. Another wave crashed, throwing her against her rescuer. He pressed his body tightly against hers to brace them against the force. Gleefully, he looked down into her eyes and unexpectedly kissed her full on the mouth. The heat from his kiss burned her cold lips.

'Come on,' he shouted, 'let's get out of here before another wave hits us.' He grabbed her hand and hauled her to safety. Someone draped a cotton blanket around her shoulders as she sat down by the fire to dry. Someone else gave her a hot dog and she realised she was hungry. From out of the darkness a bucket of fish appeared and a self-appointed chef speared each fish with a twig before handing them out to eager diners to cook over the fire.

More musicians had joined the throng, adding a heavier tone to the beat. Her rescuer handed her a beer and pulled her into some sort of staggering sway, which she presumed he classed as dancing. Everyone was on their feet dancing now, including the gathering at the Beach Bar, the atmosphere was electric. She opened her arms wide spinning around gazing up at the stars, singing at the top of her voice until she sank dizzily into the sand. She struggled up onto her elbows and looked around. A group to her right were furiously shaking their heads, swinging their long hair from side to side in time to the music. She recalled her father mentioning something about his eighteen-year-old self, partaking in a spot of head banging at rock concerts. She tried to join in, but after all the spinning and star gazing she landed flat on her back giggling helplessly.

Her rescuer threw himself down beside her. 'You look like a fallen angel lying there,' he said, his eyes glazed with alcohol and she was unsure what else.

'Have you never made a sand angel?' she laughed, flaying her arms and legs in a star shape, leaving imprints of wings in the sand. Laughing, he rolled over and planted a watery kiss at the centre of her forehead. Then staggering to his feet, he grabbed another beer and wobbled off down the beach weaving in and out of the dancers. Lydia smiled as she watched his progress across the sand. He seemed a nice person, she had enjoyed spending that moment in time with him. She sipped her beer staring into the flames, thinking of nothing in particular.

'You have the sight you know.'

Lydia snapped her head around to see who had spoken. One of the musicians, a young woman about her own age, with dark lustrous hair, had come to sit beside the fire. She studied Lydia through dark limpid eyes, a reflection of flames danced in them. Her gaze was focused, unlike the glazed expression of her fellow revellers.

'Oh, I know you think it's a curse right now, but it is a gift. Don't pretend you don't know what I'm talking about,' she said, holding up a hand. 'You're lucky to be able to see through the parallels.'

'What parallels, what do you mean?'

'The parallel worlds. The knowledge is yours to use. Don't go telling anyone, they'll not believe you and probably think you're quite mad. You are not. Don't fight it, use it. Use your mind's eye. Concentrate, you're able to see through the parallels for a reason. Look for that reason. It will be important to you.' With that, the girl stood up and sauntered over to the throng of dancers, Lydia scrambled to her feet, 'Wait!' she called after her, 'How do you know? What do you know?' The young woman simply walked on through the crowd of dancers and blended into the darkness.

Shivering, Lydia left the throng and joined her parents. No-one noticed her go.

Chapter Sixteen

'Damn the woman!' Grant said, slamming down the phone. 'Of all the times to take a vacation!' He'd been determined to get to the bottom of how Lydia Lockwood had managed to copy the Art Deco designs found in his grandfather's attic. Not only that, he'd wanted to ask her what else she knew about the history of this building. Contrary to Lydia and Jenny's assumption, he'd previously had no idea that the building was originally Barringham Hall. The sales literature had quoted Meadow Bank Hall and his legal team had dealt with the details. Now there was no doubt in his mind, that at one time, this building had been his ancestor's home. The name on the cigarette lighter that he'd found jammed at the back of his great-grandfather's desk, matched the name on the deeds and the portrait. He hadn't at first understood his obsession to buy a property in England, let alone one so derelict. Now on reflection, he thought that perhaps it was because of some long-forgotten conversation with Gramps, about his English heritage, which had planted the seed of an idea in his young brain and it had silently begun to flourish after he'd seen the derelict hall for sale on the internet. And that was another strange thing. He'd never managed to discover which agent had sent him the e-mail attaching the advertisement. Was it simply chance? There have been greater coincidences.

Whatever the motivation, Grant knew he'd been right to buy the building. Far from being a white elephant, he'd recouped much of the outlay in the first six months. It had been in his favour, that the building had been used for so many purposes over the years, people with a connection to its history, had come to visit out of sheer curiosity. He hoped they would come again to see the second phase of the renovation. That hope, brought his thoughts full circle back to Lydia. More than anything, he hoped she was genuine, despite the fact her drawings were obvious copies, he had noted the skill and flare in her work, a slight edge to the original. He aimed to have the hotel re-designed using the Art Deco style of those original designs. He'd only just acknowledged the idea to himself, but the more thought he gave to it, the more credible it seemed. Although, he hadn't voiced his idea.

He looked at the clock, it was time to set up a skype connection with his New York office. After several failed attempts, he knew he'd have to phone his personal assistant: an option he'd avoided since returning to England. Taking a deep breath, he punched in the number.

Belle answered at the first ring. 'Hi Grant, how's it going?' her warm silky tones floated into his ear from across the Atlantic, filling him with a comforting sense of home.

'Better for hearing your voice,' he said, and realised he meant it, while kicking himself for saying it. Although he and Belle had only dated from time to time, he knew she cared for him more that she was prepared to admit. They dined together informally, or went to the movies. He had bought flowers for her birthday, but hadn't offered to take her to dinner. He'd seen the hurt in her eyes, as she'd gaily told him she was celebrating with the girls.

'There's a problem with the skype this end,' she told him. 'Some guys have been working on it all morning. I've to set up a conference call. You OK to hang on there a minute? They told me to go through to the boardroom to tell them when you called. There's a whole bunch of guys working in there, blocking up all the lines.' He could picture her standing up, flicking back her dark hair. She hadn't put him on hold. She knew he hated the music. Her heels echoed into the distance provoking a ripple of desire as he thought of her long legs. She could be good fun too, he reflected, chuckling as he remembered the snowball fight they'd had in the park after she'd borrowed some kids toboggan. She'd fallen off in a tangled heap and the toboggan had descended without her. She'd jumped up with her face all aglow and eyes full of love. He'd kissed her then, slowly and tenderly, had felt her surrender to his touch. He'd wanted so much to fall in love with this beautiful girl, but he just hadn't. After that night, he'd tried to distance himself. The last thing he'd wanted was to hurt her, but his business schedule was relentless and it was all too easy to fall into her welcoming arms at the end of a gruelling day. The last time, had been the night of the electrical storms.

'You still there, Grant? OK putting you through.'

It was gone seven when Grant finished up his work. His muscles ached from sitting, so he decided to go work out in the hotel gym. He finished off with a few lengths in the pool and then relaxed in the steam room.

After dinner, he lay on the bed and watched television. Before long his eyelids drooped and he drifted into sleep. In no time at all the dream encompassed him...

The fair haired young man, was sitting up in bed reading a book. He appeared to be naked, the bed quilt covered his modesty. Grant recognised him as the young soldier in the previous dream. Candles on a bedside chest of drawers, flickered steadily, illuminating a room made gloomy by dark Victorian furniture.

One gentle tap, and the door opened a crack. Grant recognised the maid, Polly, as she slipped into the room and closed the door softly. Her hair, released from the confines of her cap, tumbled in a profusion of raven curls about her shoulders. The soft fabric of her muslin nightshift coiled enticingly around her body, revealing

121

secrets, even before her woollen shawl slipped to the ground.

Pushing back the quilt, the young man rose from the bed, confirming his nakedness. He crossed the room to where she stood shivering: whether from cold or fear, Grant couldn't be sure… The man cupped her face gently in his hands, and tenderly kissed her forehead, her cheeks, before capturing her mouth. Still she stood motionless. Lowering his gaze, he traced the column of ribbons from her throat to her breasts. Slowly he released each ribbon in turn, until all were dangling loose. His lips followed the contour of her collar bone as he slipped the nightshift from her shoulders. It landed in a white froth at her feet. His palm caressed the taught flesh of her belly and travelled upwards cupping her breast as his hungry mouth sought her lips. He cradled her head, twisting the raven curls in his fingers as he crushed her to him. Now she responded. She clasped his neck pressing her body to his, absorbing his kisses. They clung together merging as one, until, releasing her from his embrace, he lifted her up and gently cradling her in his arms he carried her to the bed. Then one by one, his gaze never leaving her face, he extinguished the candle flames, until finally the scene was plunged into darkness.

When Grant woke, the room was stifling hot. He went to turn down the radiator, but found it was stone cold. Desperate for a drink, he opened a bottle of chilled water and took it outside onto the balcony. It was not yet light. The crescent moon still hung in a black sky beside a solitary star. He replayed the dream in his head. It was linked to the previous dream and, he suddenly realised, the room had been stifling hot on that occasion as well. Now, as before, all his energy had been sapped. The last time he'd put it down to jet lag. That was not an excuse now. He sipped the water and thought of his options. His gut feeling, which had always served him well, was that Lydia and Jenny were telling the truth, even about the drawings. He instinctively felt that much more had been going on than they were prepared to tell him right now. He couldn't blame them. He was having trouble coming to terms with the coincidences himself. He decided that when Lydia returned from vacation he'd arrange a meeting with her to discuss the new refurbishment and maybe try to reach an understanding as to what influence had linked their two companies.

Chapter Seventeen

Walking through arrivals, Lydia scanned the line of taxi drivers holding up passenger name boards searching for one with her name on it. She was surprised to see Grant Stevenson standing amongst them.

'Can I give you a ride home?' he said, 'We need to talk.' He scooped up her suitcase and before she could respond, he was striding off towards the exit. He didn't speak again until they were cruising up the motorway. 'I'm sorry if I seem presumptuous turning up like this, but I really do need to talk to you.'

'What about?'

'I want you to know that I believe you.'

She turned to look at him for the first time since getting into his car. 'About all the weird stuff that's been going on?'

'Yes, about all the weird stuff.'

'What about my sketches, do you believe that I drew them from memory. Or do you still think I copied them?'

'I believe you about the sketches too. In fact, I must congratulate you. Your drawings have the edge on the originals. That's something else I wanted to talk to you about. I've decided to change the style of the hotel. I'm going to work to the original architect's plans, but I want to use your version of the original designs. I'm really impressed by your attention to detail and I think you're the best person for the job.' He waited for a response, surprised when she didn't answer straight away. 'Aren't you interested?' he said eventually.

'Of course I'm interested. I'm just surprised that's all. When did you decide all this?'

'Lydia, I need you to be honest with me. I want to know what else has been going on.'

She started to protest, but he placed a hand over hers. 'I said I believe you, because I've been having the same weird dreams, well similar anyway. Except I know that I'm asleep.' He felt her stiffen. 'No wait a minute, let me explain before you get all uptight. What I mean, is that my dreams only happen during the night. They first began soon after we found the portrait of my great-grandfather along with the deeds and drawings in Gramps attic. What I haven't told you, is that there was a second portrait, it's of my great-grandmother Lydia Fay Barringham. She looks the image of the woman you described to me as Lady Barringham, the woman who visited your shop.'

'So, she was telling the truth, she really was Lady Barringham, only from a different era, a different lifetime even. Oh, god, I feel dizzy,' she put her head between her knees.

'Are you okay honey? Would you like me to pull over onto the hard shoulder?'

'No, keep driving. I'll be alright in a minute just open the window, will you?

'There's a hip flask of whisky in the glove compartment. Take a slug of that if you think it'll help.'

She reached for the flask and poured a small measure into the lid which doubled as a cup. 'Cheers,' she said, gingerly taking a sip, 'not bad,' and she knocked back the rest of it.

'It's finest Scottish Malt whisky. It ought to be good, the price you folks charge for it over here. Look at the inscription,' he said.

She turned the flask over in her hand staring in amazement at the name Myles Barringham clearly engraved in the silver. 'Is this supposed to make feel better?'

'Sorry, I wasn't thinking.'

'Where did you get it?'

'It was found by the French polisher along with a petrol cigarette lighter stuck at the back of a drawer when the desk was being restored. Gramps gave me the desk but it had originally belonged to my great-grandfather, Myles. You feeling better now?' he said, as she sat upright in her seat.

'Yes, thank you, the whisky seems to have hit the spot. Tell me about your dreams.'

'The first one happened in America, and it focused on the derelict hall and its transformation into Art Deco. It was that first dream which seemed to plant the seed of the idea. Especially because shortly after I woke up I received an e-mail with the sales brochure for the hall attached.

You could say it was pure coincidence, but I never did track down which agent sent me that e-mail. After seeing the hall on line, it became an obsession with me. In the beginning the obsession was just to buy the building, but now the obsession has become about refurbishing it in the Art Deco style.'

'How come you went for a minimalist look then?'

'I needed a quick return on the outlay for the hall. It was the cheapest and easiest option. As it's turned out, the returns have exceeded all expectation, which is why I am now in a position to carry out my original intention. I only hope my obsession with the Art Deco restoration doesn't turn a gold mine into a white elephant.'

'I doubt that. Art Deco seems to be in vogue if my designs are anything to go by.'

'Yes, well anyway, the refurbishment was what the first two dreams were all about, but the other two dreams focused on a First World War soldier and a maid. There seems to be some sequence to them, like watching a serial drama. I think they're all set inside the hotel building, but at different times in its history.

'Frederick!' Lydia said, 'I bet the soldier was Frederick. Did you get any names?'

'Only the maid's, she was called Polly. Why, who's Frederick?'

'Frederick is Myles brother. The day before we first met you, at the hotel, Jenny and I researched the Barringham family in the local church registers with the help of the Reverend Byewaters. I was trying to find as much information as I could about the Barringham family before our meeting. I'm not altogether sure how I imagined it would help, just that if you were pulling a scam, I felt I needed as much information as I could gather on the Barringham family. I suppose I was hoping you might make a slip up if you and the mystery woman were pretending to be the Barringhams or whatever the scam was. Anyway, Myles had a brother Frederick, who was killed in France during the First World War. It just crossed my mind that you could have been dreaming about Frederick, while I've been dreaming about Myles and the lovely Lady Barringham. I've absolutely no idea why though, have you?'

'Nope, except my grandfather died recently, that's why I was in America. While we were sorting through his home, we found the portraits and the drawings in the attic. He lived in the plantation house originally owned by Myles and Lydia, and like I said, the dreams began soon after we discovered the portraits and the deeds. OK, now it's your turn. What else do you know?'

'For me, everything seems to stem from the night of the thunder storm. There hadn't been a breath of air for days and the atmosphere was sizzling with static electricity. Thunder rumbled all day and night, but the rain didn't come until just before dawn on Midsummers Eve.'

'We got the storm in the states too. It took the lights out in Manhattan.'

'Yes, I remember seeing it on the news. The night before the storm broke here, was unbearably hot. I got up for a cold drink and opened the bathroom window to try to get an air flow going. The sky was magical, it was studded with millions of stars, and a shooting star blazed a trail right across before it disappeared behind a cloud.'

'Did you make a wish?'

'Yep, and I'm not going to tell you what it was. Anyway, by that time, I was wide awake. I often find inspiration for my designs in the middle of the night, so I went down into the shop to get my sketch pad. The room was bathed in moonlight, at first it was enchanting, then the atmosphere changed. The humidity was gone, but the air was so charged with electricity I could almost hear it crackling. Then shadows began moving in the dark recesses. I thought at first it was my shadow, until I realised they were moving independently. That freaked me out I can tell you, so I switched on the light. I must have done it too quickly because the current exploded the light bulb. When I'd calmed down, I noticed that all the hats on a display had switched places. Next morning, Pippa said it would have been a customer who'd moved them, although we hadn't sold any hats that day and I don't remember seeing anyone near the display. She put them back in the correct order and then later that same day, Lady Barringham came into the shop. When she'd gone, the hats had been switched again!'

'I guess we've found one common factor,' he said,

'What's that?'

'Each time I've woken from one of those dreams; the room has been stifling hot. It was the same for you the night you went down into the shop. That was the first time you'd ever experienced any weird stuff going on, right?'

'Well yes, that's true. Do you mean the heat is generated from some form of psychic energy?'

'I don't know if I do mean that. But, now that you put it that way, I suppose...'

'We've missed one important key factor in all this talk of psychic energy. We have hard evidence in the stationery. There's the calling card and obsolete cheque, from Lady Barringham. The invitation to the ball came by post. The postman can vouch for that, I had to pay for the postage. I think the letter asking me to refurbish the hall is the creepiest though, it simply appeared on my desk. Oh! I forgot to mention that just before I found the letter, Lady Barringham materialized in the Art Deco living room window display. It was just after dawn, on the day we launched the new collection. We thought she must have got into the shop somehow and put the letter on the desk.'

'How do you mean she materialized in the window display?'

'Well the lighting and special effects have been rigged to work from a remote control. I lit the fire in the hearth first, and it was as I was messing with the dimmer switch for the lighting, that she just materialized in the fireside chair. She saluted me with a glass of Champagne. I tried to bring the lights up but the image faded away.'

'I think you just solved our mystery,' he laughed, 'we're not up against ghosts, only technology. My guess is that your first instinct was right. Someone's screwing with you. What we've got to find out, is who, and why they're so hell bent on connecting you to the hotel and my ancestors.'

'What do you mean only technology?'

'Apparitions, they're easy to conjure up. There are some very sophisticated systems on the market well capable of projecting hologram ghosts and women in arm chairs. Someone's tampered with the remote. What company did you use to install the system?'

'That's Jenny's department, I'll have to check. But Lady Barringham looked pretty 3D solid to me.'

'Oh I think we'll find she's real enough. There's someone out there doing a convincing impersonation. Tell me, was she wearing that same yellow dress each time that you've seen her, including the time you saw her in the shop window?'

'Yes, come to think of it she was. I suppose it would be easy to get a wig in that classic bob. No wonder it looked so perfect. I've been envious of that hair for months,' she said, patting her own curly hair. 'And you can get non-prescription coloured lenses now. But if as you say, the portraits and documents were in America until quite recently, where is she getting her information from. The detail is quite specific.'

'That's what we've got to find out.'

'Yes, but that still doesn't answer why we're having the dreams though, does it?'

'Have you ever heard of auto-suggestion? We'll have to check for bugs. At a certain point in sleep our brain is susceptible to suggestion. Maybe someone's talking us through the visualization, then when we wake, it seems real.'

'This is England not America. I think you're getting carried away with all this hi-tech stuff.'

'Where do you think half this stuff was invented? Anyway, I think we should run it by the local police.'

He parked the car outside the shop then turned to look at her. 'So, I can count on you as interior designer for the project, right? I've to arrange a meeting with the architects. What day would suit you best?'

'Monday's are a safe bet, I can usually keep my diary clear then, it's my day off.'

'I know what that feels like, working a day off,' he laughed. 'Come on, I'll give you a hand with your bags.'

Pippa was waiting in the shop doorway, 'Hello,' she said. 'I've made a surprise dinner to welcome you home. It will be ready in five minutes.' She smiled up at Grant, 'It'll stretch to another one?'

'You'll be missing a treat if you don't stay,' Lydia laughed. 'She's an ace cook.' Assuming he'd accept, she made her way across the shop and up the stairs to her apartment. Half way up, she stopped and turned, 'Thank you for believing in me,' she said.

Caught off balance, Grant was toppled backwards by the weight of the suitcase. Instinctively she grabbed out for him, he's so like Myles, she thought, gazing into his sparkling blue eyes. Then his eyes darkened and he kissed her. She pressed closer, felt the hardness of his toned body, heard his low moan and her passion soared to match his. The suitcase bounced noisily off each step, until it lay discarded at the foot of the stairs.

'Red wine or white?' Lydia spun around to see Nick James standing at the top of the stairs.

'Not for me thanks,' Grant said, dropping down the stairs to retrieve the case. 'I've a long drive back. I'll be in touch,' he said to Lydia. Then he dropped the case at Nick's feet and ran back down the stairs. The door slammed behind him and the little bell over the door tinkled long into the silence that followed.

The meal was strained, worsened by Pippa's all too bright attempt at keeping the conversation going. When Lydia announced that she had a headache and was going to bed, the relief in the room was tangible. Nick offered to take Pippa home.

'Thank you, that's kind,' Lydia said. She turned to Pippa and gave her a hug 'Now I won't worry about you getting home safely. Thank you again for a lovely meal.' She was surprised to see Nick look pointedly at Pippa with one eyebrow raised and Pippa blush furiously before averting her eyes, but Lydia felt too tired to try and decipher their interaction.

Chapter Eighteen

Lydia's feigned headache of the previous evening had developed into a full-blown migraine during the night. The sickening thump in her head as she sat up in bed made her stomach lurch. God, why is migraine so much like a hangover without the pleasure of getting drunk? she thought, taking her pills from the bathroom cabinet. She ran the cold tap for a glass of water and winced at the sight of herself. She heard the shop door being unlocked and poked her head out of the bathroom to look at the kitchen clock. Too early for customers, so she padded downstairs in her slippers and dressing gown.

'Not feeling any better then?' Pippa said, 'You look like death warmed up.'

'I feel like it. Look I've got a two o'clock appointment, do you think you can cope if I go back to bed for the morning?'

When the alarm clock woke her several hours later, she felt much better although the dull ache in her head had not completely gone. After a shower, coffee and toast, she was ready to set off for her appointment. She pulled up outside the client's house a good half hour early. She didn't perceive that to be a problem until she discovered there was no-one home. As she climbed back in the car, her mobile rang. It was Grant Stevenson. 'Hi, how you doing? Look I know this is short notice, but I've an architect coming to talk over the plans at around five. I know you said Mondays were best for you, but he was in the neighbourhood and had a cancellation.'

'I'm at a client's quite near to you. I should be able to make it there by five.'

'Sweet, see you then.'

There was still no sign of her client, so she decided to go over the proposals while she waited. As she pulled the paper work from her brief case an unfamiliar piece of parchment came out with it. She spread the small document across the steering wheel. It appeared to be a part of Grant's original architect's drawings for Barringham Hall. How on earth had it got inside the briefcase? Fascinated, she was soon completely engrossed, lost in her imagination, as she mentally walked along the corridors and through the rooms she'd seen, guided by Myles.

Automatically, she began jotting down ideas, adding her own flare.

'I like your designs. Will you help me, Lydia?' She spun around expecting to see Myles sitting in the back seat. She was completely alone. Someone banged on the car window and she jumped sending her papers flying. 'Gosh you startled me!' she said, winding down the window to hear what her client was saying.

'I'm so sorry, only I didn't want you to drive off. I thought you might be thinking that I'd forgotten our appointment. I had to collect my son early from school, he's not well.'

Lydia looked at the crest fallen child turning a deeper shade of green by the minute. 'Of course, you must see to your son first,' she said, worried that the child might be sick all over her car. 'You go ahead and I'll take my time gathering my things together.'

The appointment went well, and the client, anxious to see to her child, hadn't kept Lydia talking as most people were apt to do. Walking down the path she glanced at her watch. Plenty of time to get to the hotel before the architect arrived. She was fastening her seat belt when she heard the voice again.

'He needs your support. You've a battle on your hands, the pair of you.' She looked in the rear-view mirror. The back seat was empty.

Forty minutes later, she pulled into the hotel car park. Climbing out of the car she glanced up at Grant's apartment. He was standing in the window speaking on the phone. He must have been watching out, he waved. She returned the wave and made her way inside.

He greeted her in reception. 'The architect guy's already here,' he said, holding open a door onto a long corridor. 'He's in the office at the end.'

An hour into negotiations, Lydia reflected that whoever had spoken to her in the car had predicted correctly. She and Grant certainly had a fight on their hands. The architect seemed to find fault from every angle. He had a reputation for his unique talent, so Grant had told her. Lydia decided his talent and interest in their project stretched as far as making himself a fast buck.

By seven o'clock Lydia and Grant were sitting in a secluded corner of the dining room having ended the meeting somewhere on common ground. Out of respect for her lingering headache and the drive home, Lydia sipped sparkling water, even though Grant had assured her the wine selection had improved greatly in recent months.

'You know what that architect's problem is, don't you?' she said, looking across the table at Grant. 'Those plans need craftsmen who are skilled in period restoration. They're in small supply and high demand. They'll be expensive.'

'That's not a problem, we've discussed the finance.'

'Yes, but I'll be surprised if he carries his own team of craftsmen with the necessary skills to do this job. So, if the craftsmen are self-employed, he'll have to submit their invoices, which means he won't be able to cream a bit off the top for himself.'

'You're not just a pretty face, are you?' he chuckled. 'His was the most expensive quote, but he came highly recommended. I didn't involve you with the others because I'd already decided to use him. But you're right, sometimes the obvious choice isn't the good one. This project's going to be complicated enough, without arguing with the architect at every stage. I'll look elsewhere.'

Over dinner, it was inevitable that the conversation came around to the mystery that had brought them together. 'What I find curious,' Lydia said, 'is that if someone is bugging our apartments and using auto suggestion technique, how come I interact in my dreams where as you're an observer?'

'I guess that's just how individual brains function. I'm glad you reminded me, I think I'll run our theory by the police in the morning. What about the guy you live with, what does he think about it all?'

'What guy? I live alone.'

'When I gave you a ride home from the airport, there was a guy in your apartment.'

'Oh, you mean Nick. He's the local vet, and I've no idea what he was doing there. I've had a couple of drinks with him, but it was no big deal. We never arranged another date or anything.' She was intrigued to see the glimmer of a smile, expertly disguised, tugging at the corner of his mouth. 'I'd better get going,' she said, folding her napkin. 'It'll be late when I get back and I've to collect my dog yet.'

'Why don't you call the dog minder and bed down here for the night? We're a hotel, plenty of spare beds.'

She saw a devilish glint in his eye. If her head didn't ache so much, she might just have been tempted. But as it was, she stood up and held out her hand. 'Thank you for dinner.'

'A pleasure doing business with you,' he said, holding on to her hand a fraction too long.

Grant Stevenson watched the tail lights of Lydia's car cruise down the drive and out of sight. He felt ridiculously happy that she didn't live with the vet. Now all he had to contend with was his great-grandfather. Ghost, hologram, whatever. Grant was certain he had a rival for Lydia's affections in his ancestor.

Chapter Nineteen

The journey home was uneventful. Lydia collected Billy, then after playing with him in the garden for a while, went to bed. She woke refreshed from a dreamless sleep full of ideas for re-designing the hotel into the Art Deco style. She had also thought of the perfect event to launch the re-opening after the refurbishment was complete.

Her enthusiasm to get on with it all was soon sidelined by an onslaught of customers. To make matters worse, at the height of the rush, a couple of plain clothes men sent by the police turned up to check for bugging devices in the shop and apartment. To cap it all, they took the remote to bits on the counter, just as she was boxing up a dress, and she had to defer to the workroom. After an hour, they left without saying a word.

It was a week later before Lydia's plans had crystalized and then she phoned Grant.

'A garden party?' he sounded unimpressed.

'Yes, but no ordinary garden party. A vintage one.' There was silence at the other end of the phone. 'OK, hear me out. I've based the whole theme around the dream I had of the cricket match. I've included the minutest detail right down to the cucumber sandwiches and fly covers over the milk jugs.'

'Honey, I'm American, I have no idea what you're talking about.'

'Yes of course. I keep forgetting. Your accent comes and goes.'

'English nanny. It's a family thing.'

'Well trust me. A garden party and an afternoon of cricket, is just the sort of vintage event you need to promote the new image. Why don't you come over for dinner one night and I can show you my sketches?'

'Now there's an offer I can't refuse.'

'Yes, well don't get your hopes up,' she said, ignoring the double entendre. 'My cooking's not in Pippa's league.'

It was almost Christmas when Grant came to see her sketches. The tree reached the ceiling and filled one corner of the living room where it twinkled merrily beside a roaring log burner. One of her regular customers had brought her a gammon joint spiked with cloves, and another had made mince pies. Both were warming in the oven circulating their spicy scent.

'I hope you like mulled wine,' she said, greeting him at the kitchen door with a glass mug full of it in her hand.

'That's an interesting route to take,' he said, looking back down the steps. 'I felt like a burglar sneaking in the back way.'

'Yes, sorry about that,' she said, taking a sip of the hot wine. 'I'm used to it now. It saves opening the shop and messing about with two different codes. I've had alarms fitted since all your talk of people bugging the place. Dinner will be another half an hour.'

'Smells delicious, I brought a bottle of red and a liqueur I tried recently, which is rather delicious too.'

'Cheers,' she said, putting her mug of wine down on the worktop before taking the bottles. 'There's a cloakroom in the hall where you can hang your coat. If you go through to the living room, you'll find the sketches on the coffee table, I'll join you in a minute.'

'It's looking very festive in here. It makes me feel kinda home sick.'

Dinner was a success, they talked over the sketches and outlined a plan as to how they might work, given the limited space in the hotel grounds.

'Go and sit on the sofa, it's more comfortable,' Lydia said, getting up to check on the percolator. She returned with a tray stacked with coffee, mince pies and liqueurs. Grant moved the sketches so she could put it down.

'So, you were born in America?' she said, sipping the coffee laced with the liqueur, 'but had an English nanny?'

'Governess really. A family tradition my great-grandfather wasn't prepared to relinquish even though he'd left England for America. That, and boarding school. I'd have preferred to stay around the ranch, but my own father insisted on boarding school as well. I guess I'm grateful in the long run.'

'Tell me, what do you know about your great-grandparents?'

'Only what Gramps told me. They eloped from England to America. All they had were Lydia's jewels,'

'Lydia's. They weren't Myles' jewels then?'

'No, her grandmother left them to her. Why?'

'It was something Reverend Byewaters said. Rumour has it, Myles stole the family jewels before he disappeared.'

'Not according to my family and the jewels were never sold. Lydia and Myles got jobs instead, as interpreters at the pawn brokers shop where they'd tried to sell them. My mother wears them occasionally.'

'But he can't have made his fortune interpreting for a pawn broker, surely.'

'Not quite. Both he and Lydia were fluent in French and Myles also spoke German. Something to do with the First World War, not sure what. Anyway, while they worked, they learned about the people travelling through the busy port and more importantly, what those people most needed. Once they'd saved enough money, Myles opened a general store with good quality, cheap accommodation above. Lydia discovered that women were arriving regularly in the port, having sailed with their kid's half way around the world to meet a husband who'd gone on ahead supposedly to prepare the way for his family. Only the truth of it was that many of the women discovered when they docked, that their husband had deserted them. Then those women, driven by the need to feed their kids, became vulnerable to all kinds of vices.'

'It doesn't bear thinking about, does it?' Lydia said. 'It would be bad enough finding yourself alone in a strange country, let alone having responsibility for your children.'

'That's what Lydia and Myles must have thought, because they opened a second store with accommodation as a refuge for women and children. It was intended to put them on until they'd found legitimate employment to support themselves, or made enough money to pay for a passage back home.'

'They sound like truly kind people to me. Myles doesn't come across at all like the black sheep the Reverend was talking about.'

'I don't know about that, but he certainly had a nose for business. Gramps inherited it, and it seems I have too. You know the one thing that impresses me most about Myles? It's not the fact that he owned a string of stores, or a hotel and night club as well as the plantation. It's the fact that he managed to bring every single one of his employees safely through the Wall Street crash and the depression that followed. Now that's one hell of a guy... hey are you alright?' he said, seeing the tears well up in her eyes.

'Yes, yes I'm fine, it was an emotional story, that's all,' she said, hiding the true reason for her tears. She had been right all along to believe in Myles. He was a good man. She kept her thoughts to herself, she knew he wasn't a dream or a figment of her imagination. He certainly wasn't a hologram. He was warm and real.

'It's getting late,' she said to Grant,

'Yes, you're right, I'd better be making tracks as Gramps would say. It was icing over on the way here. I'll need to keep it steady on the way back. Thank you for dinner and thanks again for those sketches. Great idea. I'll be in touch.' He shrugged into his coat and bent down to kiss her cheek.

'Have a safe journey,' she said, opening the door. An icy blast hit them.

'I'll be making tracks alright,' he said, standing in the doorway. 'I reckon I've got a problem. That snow looks at least ten centimetres deep; it will be twice as deep outside the village. The chassis on my car is too low to ride over it. If the forecast had predicted snow, I'd have brought the Range Rover'

'In that case. You're welcome to use my spare room.'

'I guess I'll have to take you up on that. It's not as though I can walk!' It was the wrong thing to say. Billy hearing his favourite command, raced to the door and cannoned into the back of Grant's legs. Grant spun around trying to regain his balance, but slipped off the kitchen step, and landed in a heap in the snow.

'Oh dear, I'm so sorry, are your hurt?' she said, laughing too much to help him up.

A snow ball whizzed past her left ear. It landed with a plop on the kitchen floor. She scooped up a handful of snow from the step and took aim.

Grant rolled away as it sailed past. 'Truce,' he shouted, jumping up.

Billy was exploring in the garden. With his nose to the ground, he weaved and zigzagged along, eagerly following the scent trails of animals scurrying home to their burrows. He seemed overjoyed. It was the first time in his young life that he'd experienced snow. Clusters of snow dangled from the tips of his ears sparkling like opals, they danced merrily as he barked.

'I don't think we've much choice, do you? We're going for a walk, whether we want to or not. I have boots in the back of the car. How about you?'

'I'll find my wellies.'

Ten minutes later, they were kitted out and romping through the park, like a pair of school children. One snowball hit Grant squarely on the jaw. 'I'll get you for that!' he laughed, and wrestled her to the floor, pinning her arms above her head. He kissed her, smack on the lips, then rolled over onto his back.

'What are you doing?' she asked.

'Making snow angels!'

'Oh, I'm very good at making those,' she giggled, feeling quite intoxicated by the moment and an abundance of mulled wine…

The next moment he was taking her hands and hauling her up. Startled she opened her eyes and the laughter froze on her lips, as she stared into Myles face.

She looked around. She was still in the park, but the scene had changed. The ice-covered branches now sparkled beneath the glow of gas lamps, and flare torches lined the path. The vandalized bandstand was restored to its former glory and the band, though heavily muffled against the winter's night, played valiantly on for skaters waltzing around the frozen lake. The circumference of the lake was lined with vendors selling their wares from handcarts beside braziers filled with red hot coals, roasting potatoes and chestnuts, as well as providing warmth. A long queue had formed beside a cart roasting a hog and there was an equally long queue of people waiting to dip the brassier poker into their glass of beer, to warm it up. The delicious smell of roasting food mingling with the smell of warm hops made Lydia feel hungry again. But there was no time to linger. Myles was pulling her towards a park bench. 'Do hurry up old bean. I thought you were never going to get here!' he said, shoving a pair of skates into her hand.

'I can't skate,' she protested, but Myles was already removing her Wellington boots and replacing them with the skates. 'Nothing to it, dear girl. Come on,' and taking her arm he pulled her to a shaky stance, then wrapping his other arm around her waist, he guided her onto the ice.

After they'd made their third lap around the lake, she felt she was beginning to get the hang of skating. She realised how mistaken she was when Myles let go and she landed on her bottom with her legs sticking out like a china doll.

'Not a natural at this, old girl, are you?' he said, hauling her up, Lydia's feet began to part company, she flung herself backwards to prevent doing the side splits and Myles almost toppled with her. He crushed her against his chest to right them both. She looked up into his eyes, about to make some witty quip expecting to see the usual mischief lurking there. Instead she was amazed to see him looking at her with such love, that tears sprang to her eyes. She kissed him then with a passion she hadn't known she possessed. She kissed him for all the loves she'd known and lost. She kissed him for all the confusion and hurt that knowing him had caused her. She kissed him for the desolation she had felt when her parents had emigrated. But most of all she kissed him because…god help her, apparition or not, she was madly and hopelessly, completely in love with him. They clung together in the centre of the frozen lake and Lydia felt his restrain as though battling some inner struggle. Whether it was social etiquette or some other turmoil, she was unsure, but she felt him fight the battle and surrender. She rejoiced in the exquisite moment his resolve crumbled and his lips responded, searching and probing the sensitive flesh of her mouth, skilful and enticing, promising a joy beyond all comprehension.

A piercing wolf whistle, brought them back to reality. 'If yah hungry mister, yah can get a hot tattie over there!' a cheeky lad skating by called out.

'Oh, I beg your pardon; I do apologise, despicable behaviour on my part.'

'It wasn't your fault, it was mine, and I've no intention of apologizing.'

'Cheeky young whipper snapper,' Myles shouted, shaking his fist mockingly at the lad's retreating figure.

'Come on,' she said, satisfied that his good humour was restored, 'I need a hot chocolate.' Linking, her arm through his, they skated off the ice.

She stood leaning against a tree with her mittened hands cupping a mug of cocoa, 'What?'

she said, sensing him looking at her, 'have I got cocoa on my top lip?'

'No,' he smiled, shaking his head. He caught a strand of her hair and tucked it under her hat. 'I was thinking that you look like an angel fallen to earth with your face all aglow and your golden curls escaping at odd angles from your hat.'

'Angel?' she smiled…The scene faded and she was lying on her back making a snow angel.

She scrambled to her feet and looked all around. She expected Grant to ask where she'd been, but he was still laughing and flapping his arms and legs up and down making a snow angel as though only seconds had past.

The joy slipped from his face as he looked up and saw her standing shivering infront of him. 'What is it, are you cold?'

Back at the flat, Lydia sipped the brandy Grant had poured, and watched him stoke up the fire. She had told him about everything, except the kiss. She hugged that to herself. In any case, if she was to develop any sort of a relationship with him, that piece of information wasn't exactly going to spur things along. The song 'Dream Lover' popped into her head. If Myles was indeed a dream, then it was possible to have the best of both worlds.

Grant came to sit beside her on the sofa, 'The brandy's put some colour back in your cheeks. Feeling better?'

'Much better, thank you,' she said, setting down the glass, and she leaned in to kiss him. His response was instant; the kiss was as she remembered. All her pent-up tension drained away and she was floating. Abruptly the kissing stopped. 'What's wrong?'

'Nothing's wrong,' he said, cupping her face and searching her eyes. 'It's just that a working relationship, alongside a romantic one, can be tricky. I want us to be sure that we aren't getting into something we can't handle.' He stood up, 'How about I make us some coffee?'

Left alone, she leaned back against the sofa and tried to calm her emotions. She heard Grant set the percolator going and then she heard him on the phone to his hotel night staff, asking for a volunteer to drive over in the Range Rover to come and pick him up. When he came back through with the coffee, she was curled up in a ball on the sofa, feigning sleep. He covered her with the duvet from her bed, she could smell her night cream on it. Then he sat down in the chair beside the fire to drink his coffee.

Before he left, he planted a kiss on her forehead. 'A real-life snow angel,' he said, and walked out through the kitchen, closing the back door softly behind him.

How strange, she thought, snuggling further under the duvet, that both men in my life should compare me to an angel, and she fell asleep with a sweet smile.

Chapter Twenty

Lydia woke with a start. For a moment, she couldn't think why she was sleeping on the sofa. Then everything came flooding back and she groaned as she remembered how Grant had abruptly pulled away moments after she'd begun kissing him. It had never been her style to take the initiative. After last night's embarrassment, it never would. Then she remembered kissing Myles and let the bitter sweet memory wash over her.

She went through to the kitchen and opened the back door for Billy, then made a cup of tea. She drank it watching him through the window cavorting about in the snow. How uncomplicated his world seemed, so long as he'd been walked, fed and watered, he was content to keep her company or sleep in his bed. She cleaned out his bowls and put down a fresh supply of food and water. He was still engrossed in tracking scents around the garden, so she left him to it and headed off to the bathroom. On the way, she heard voices coming from the shop. She recognised Pippa's voice, but then a man's voice interrupted. It was Nick James'. What on earth was he doing here at this hour? She stopped to listen.

'You'll have to tell her you know.'

'I will, but in my own time. I haven't had the opportunity, that's all.'

'I don't see what the big deal is. There was never anything between us. We just had a couple of drinks together.'

Lydia had absolutely no idea what they were talking about. But an uneasy knot formed in her stomach. Whatever it was, it must be very important. She'd trust Pippa with her life, so she felt sure it must be something Pippa was only trying to protect her from. Whether it was to do with the business or a personal matter, she felt hurt that Pippa was finding it difficult to talk to her.

When she went downstairs, Nick James was nowhere to be seen. Jenny and Pippa were huddled together looking at a book. They snapped the book shut and jumped apart as she walked into the shop. She gave the book a cursory glance, it was one of the shop's own catalogues. 'I'll be in the office when you've got a minute,' she said. 'There's a new project I want to talk to you about.'

'I'll bring some coffee through,' Pippa said, and Jenny followed Lydia into the office.

'I won't keep you long. I had dinner with Grant Stevenson last night.'

'How did it go?' Jenny said, raising an eyebrow.

'We discussed my designs, and ideas for a launch to promote the hotel once the Art Deco makeover is finished.'

'Let's get it started first,' Jenny groaned.

'The makeover's what I wanted to speak to you about as well. Would you be prepared to oversee it, if I do the launch?'

'You know I'd jump at the chance. But it's always been your project. What's up?'

'I've overstretched my work schedule.'

'Then let me take over some of your other clients. I'm sure Grant Stevenson would prefer you on his team.'

'But you wouldn't object to taking over?'

'No, I'd be delighted to, if you're sure that's what you want.' The door-bell jingled announcing a customer. 'I'll get that,' she said, almost colliding with Pippa in the doorway.

Later that day, Grant Stevenson turned up unexpectedly. Lydia invited him into the office and closed the door.

'If you ask me,' Jenny said, jerking her head towards the office, 'something's gone off between those two.'

'I think you're right. I was so sure she liked him that I was going to tell her my news today,' Pippa said, 'now I don't know what to do.'

'You can't run your own life to suit other people you know.'

A short while later, Grant walked out of the office. 'Back in a minute,' he said, 'I've got to move my car, the parking time's out.'

'Go on, now's your chance,' Jenny said, giving Pippa a shove. 'Nip in while he's moving his car. You've the perfect excuse to escape when he comes back,'

Pippa froze in the doorway when she saw that Lydia had the bridal catalogue open on the desk.

'Just the person,' Lydia smiled up at her. 'There's an order sticker on this page but I don't have an order to go with it. Do you know anything about it?'

'No, I mean, yes, I mean I'll look at it later,' and she made to leave.

'Pippa is anything wrong? Did you come in to talk to me about something?'

'Yes, but it will keep for another time.'

'Now's a good time for me.'

'No honestly its fine,' She turned and crashed into Grant.

'Whoa there, honey! You OK?' She nodded and fled to the workroom.

'I have no idea what's got into her today. Did you get the chance to speak to Jenny?'

Before he could reply, the shop door burst open and Nick James staggered in with a crate of Champagne. 'Congratulations are in order,' he shouted, slamming the crate down on the counter. Hearing all the commotion, everyone gathered in the shop. Pippa was the last to come through from the workroom.

'I'm getting married,' he said, smiling across at Pippa and holding out his hand. 'This is my beautiful bride to be.' He wrapped his arms around her and kissed her. A huge cheer when up from the workroom girls and everyone began clapping and congratulating them at once.

'Bring the Champagne in here will you Nick, we've tidied the work away for today.'

He dutifully carried the crate through to the workroom and soon corks were popping and Champagne was overflowing from the paper cups that one of the workroom girls had found in a cupboard.

When all the fuss had died down, Pippa managed to talk to Lydia. 'You don't mind, do you?'

'I'm delighted! Why should I mind?'

'Well, you saw him first type of thing.'

'Pippa, I had a couple of drinks with the guy. You two are perfect for each other, go and be happy.'

'Thank you,' she said, giving Lydia a hug. 'Oh, and you know that order sticker in the bridal book? Well that's me. Well the base of the style. I'll go over my design with you tomorrow if you would like to see it.'

'Can't wait,' Lydia said, lifting her cup of Champagne. 'Now go and enjoy yourself.'

Grant came over and topped up her Champagne, 'Did you really not know about the engagement?' he asked.

'Hadn't a clue.'

'So, you won't know that they intend getting married at the hotel.'

'Let's hope the refurbishments finished then.'

'Look, have you handed the project over to Jenny because of what happened last night?'

'Maybe.'

'Does maybe mean that you're interested in developing the romantic side of our partnership?'

'Grant I'm sorry, I really can't talk about this right now.'

The workroom cleared as people began to leave for home. Jenny stacked the empty bottles back into the crate and Pippa stood beside Nick, twisting her left hand this way and that, admiring the stones in her ring as they flashed under the bright lighting.

'We're having dinner at the Italian in the village if anyone wants to join us,' Nick said. Everyone declined, and his relief was evident in the way he was gazing at Pippa.

Grant was the last to leave, and just as Lydia was about to lock the shop door after him, he turned around and came back. 'I almost forgot to say what I originally came to see you about.'

'Will it take long? 'Do you want to go through to the office?' If he was surprised that she hadn't invited him up to the apartment, he didn't let it show.

'That depends on you,' he sighed, giving the impression he was sick of humouring her. 'The police got back to me. They didn't find any bugging devices in either of our apartments. The remote for the window display hadn't been tampered with either. So, where do you think that leaves us?'

'It leaves me needing a black coffee. Do you want one?' she said, heading for her apartment after all.

Billy fussed them as they entered the kitchen and Lydia opened the door so he could play in the garden.

'I still believe there's a logical explanation for all this.' Grant said, 'If the apartments were bugged, someone probably knew we were calling in the police. They must have taken the bugs out again before the police came.'

'And the dreams?'

'We only have our own interpretation of their meaning. Look at the facts Lydia. I've just lost the man who was perhaps my greatest influence. Gramps was much more to me than a grandparent. He was real proud of his English heritage. I'm convinced that's the reason I bought the derelict hall. The fact that I decided to hold a Roaring Twenty's Ball must have been like a beacon for a business head like yours.'

'Yes alright, you make it sound so simple when you dissect it like that. But it's not so simple when you have ghostly apparitions cavorting in the darkness, or when you're perfectly happy making snow angels one minute and then skating around a frozen lake a hundred years earlier the next.'

'Cheers,' he said, taking the freshly percolated coffee. 'Well at least humour me. Let's get in a private investigator. They might just come up with something, they'll have the time to dig a bit deeper.'

'Yes, you're right,' she said. 'I'm sure the police feel they've more important issues to spend their resources on than ghost busting.'

'I'm certain of it,' he laughed. 'I'd better get going, I'll be in touch.' He left by the back way, spending a few moments throwing snow balls for Billy to chase, before slipping through the gate.

Lydia went down into the garden and shot the bolt across on the gate. 'Come on in, Billy. It's too cold to stay out here.' She was glad extra lighting had been added to her new security system.

After the flurry of pre-Christmas shoppers had died down, Lydia took some time off and walked Billy to the newsagents to buy stamps for her cards. She tied him up outside and made her way to the post office section. As usual Mrs. T. was in the mood for a chat. 'Have you seen that poster in the window, the one about that lady private investigator? Natalie Jacobs, she's called.'

Lydia stuck the stamps on her Christmas cards while she listened to Mrs. T. chattering on and then handed them over for posting. 'Is she for real do you think, this Natalie Jacobs?'

'I expect so. She's retired CID, so she says.'

The next evening, flicking through the local paper, Lydia came across an article on Natalie Jacobs. The image was far removed from how she had imagined her. Dark eyes, skilfully made up, stared out from an oval face. Her black hair was brushed back and secured in a French plait, the end of which was peeping over one shoulder.

Lydia picked up the phone and dialled Grant. 'I've just found our private investigator. See if you can pick up a copy of the evening paper from reception and give me a call back.'

'What makes you think I haven't got one?'

'Do you have one?'

'No. I'll call you back.'

Chuckling, Lydia was about to put down the phone, when it rang.

'Hi, it's me,' Pippa said, 'Do you think Grant would like to come with you to Christmas lunch?'

'I'll ask him. I'm waiting for him to phone me back. Have you looked at the evening paper?'

'Not yet, why?'

'There's an article on a private investigator. It's very interesting. You should have a look if you get time.'

'So, you're definitely going down the investigator route then?'

'Yes. It was Grant's idea really, but I agree with him that it's better to do something about the problem rather than just ignoring it.

'I'm sure it is. Let me know what he says about Christmas. See you tomorrow.'

An hour went by before Grant returned her call. 'Sorry, got caught up in something.'

'What do you think?' she said.

'Well I sure wasn't expecting a private investigator to look like that,' he laughed.

'Me neither, but she sounds experienced. Do you think we should contact her after the holidays?'

'Yes, for sure. And speaking of the holidays have you got anything planned?'

'I'm going to spend Christmas day with Pippa and her family. Nick will be there of course, and she's invited you, if you'd like to come.'

'Sounds good, especially if she cooks as great as you say. Do I need to bring anything other than booze?'

'I'll ask Pippa.'

'Are you free Christmas Eve? There's a gala dinner on here and I've hired a cabaret act.

I'd like it if you'd join me for dinner. Santa will be dropping by and if you've been a good girl, he might just bring you a present.'

'I'd like that,' she laughed, 'Will you book me a room? It will be easier to go straight from there to Pippa's.'

Christmas Eve dawned with the kind of deep orange sun that heralds blue skies and a crisp dry day. Lydia clipped on Billy's lead and they set off for the park. She was pleased the shop was already closed for the holidays. They played in the woods; Billy chasing squirrels and sticks, then after a jog around the lake they returned home for a hearty breakfast.

After breakfast, Lydia carefully laid the presents on the back seat of the car beside an overnight bag. Billy jumped into the boot and they set off. The roads were clear and she arrived ahead of time. Grant was already waiting, he walked down the steps to greet her as she climbed out of the car. 'Your patio door key,' he said, 'the doggy suite is situated at the bottom end of the garden and dogs have to use the patio doors to come and go.'

She took the key from him and let Billy out of the boot. 'Would you mind giving me a hand with Billy's bed? I can manage the case. I'll come back for the presents.'

The room was surprisingly plush for a dog friendly suite. Billy worked busily, sniffing out every nook and cranny, then, satisfied that the room met with his approval, he flopped down in his bed and went to sleep.

'He seems to have settled in. Would you like some lunch? We can take him out for a walk again before dinner.'

Lunch was delightful. It appeared in the form of afternoon tea, plates of dainty sandwiches, cakes and warm mince pies with rum sauce on the side. A choir sang carols and Christmas songs, before passing round a collection tin, in aid of a local hospice.

After lunch, they wrapped up warmly and set off on a tour of the gardens. It soon became apparent that her plans for the garden party would need to be scaled down.

Set well away from the hotel and main gardens was a small copse. Billy scampered off in its direction on the hunt for squirrels and soon disappeared between the trees. They followed on at a more leisurely pace. At the centre of the copse was a square sandstone building. Two fluted pillars either side of the door supported a triangular portico.

'Oh, my god it's a crypt,' Lydia's hand flew to her mouth. The sun had sunk low in the sky and the bare branches creaked and groaned as the wind picked up. The sandstone was blackened by years of pollution and splattered white with bird droppings. It was a forlorn, desolate structure.

Billy came crashing through the undergrowth to join them. He thumped his tail against Grant's leg and looked up happily at Lydia with his tongue lolling to one side; clearly, he hadn't picked up on an atmosphere.

'There's an engraving on the portico. It's in Latin. Not my best subject in school.'

'Perhaps Reverend Byewaters can translate it. He seems as keen on the Barringham family as we are.'

Bored with standing around, Billy scampered off again and Lydia, glad to get away, followed him. 'When did you find out that the crypt was there?' she asked, as they walked back to the hotel.

'It's listed on the paper work, but the gardeners told me about it. The copse provides a natural screen.'

'Do you know who's in there?'

'No, maybe that's another question we could ask the Reverend.'

That evening, Lydia made a special effort with her hair and make-up and in a devil, may care moment, put on the Lady Barringham dress. She knew she'd made the right choice, when she saw the expression on Grant's face.

The evening was relaxed and festive. Dinner was outstanding and the cabaret act Grant had promised turned out to be a complete floor show, with dancers, singers and a very good comedienne. Santa delivered everyone a gift as promised. 'Thank you,' Lydia said, unwrapping a slim silver bangle. It glinted in the light as she slipped it over her hand, 'It's very pretty.'

'Nothing to do with me,' he laughed. 'Look around, all the ladies have a bangle from Santa. The guys have a pen.'

She could see now that each lady had an identical bracelet. She also noticed that several women were wearing her creations, unlike the last time she'd been in this room. She smiled remembering the hilarious party games they'd played and how she'd been impressed that Myles could dance the Charleston. She hadn't known then, that he was…

'Do you dance?' she suddenly asked.

'Of course, would you like to?' The band was playing a slow foxtrot and she smiled up at him as he gathered her close to lead her into the dance. Grant was good for her she realised. He shared her sense of humour, and so far, they'd agreed on most of their business decisions.

It was after midnight when she unlocked the patio door. She whistled Billy to come outside for his last run. The North Star shone brightly in the dark sky. She thought back to the night of the storms. Had it been coincidence or had all her troubles begun with a stupid wish on a shooting star. She shivered in the frosty air.

'Merry Christmas, honey,' Grant said, wrapping his arms around her. He kissed her softly and she melted against him. His kisses grew more urgent, probing, searching. 'Come inside,' she whispered, taking his hand. She locked the door and drew the curtains. It was as she turned that she saw the small gift wrapped package sitting on the pillow. Smiling at Grant she crossed the room and picked it up. 'Thank you, Merry Christmas.'

'I'm sorry, I didn't get you that one either.'

'Well then who did?' she pulled at the ribbon and gasped as she opened the box. There, dazzling against a cushion of black velvet, sat an exquisite diamond and platinum brooch made in the Art Deco image of a shooting star. Attached to it was a familiar guilt-edged card, inscribed with the words, Merry Christmas Lydia, with fondest love, MB x

It was just over a week into the New Year that Natalie Jacobs sat facing Lydia Lockwood of Deco Designs, and thought with increasing certainty that she was speaking to a madwoman. Either that or she was at the centre of some sort of practical joke. Yet despite her misgivings, by the end of the meeting, she was convinced that the group gathered in the small office believed they were telling her the truth. Retired DCI Natalie Jacobs had done her research into Ms. Lockwood and her Art Deco design company prior to the meeting and had been impressed. She prided herself on being a good judge of character, and her gut instinct was telling her that however ludicrous it seemed, she must treat the information seriously. On a practical level, she couldn't afford not to. She needed the money. Becoming a private investigator hadn't been such a smart move after all. Up until now people hadn't taken her agency or her skills seriously.

'Well, I've enough information to be going on with,' she said, reciting the standard reply which meant she hadn't a clue what she was going to do with it. 'I'll be in touch again in a couple of weeks. In the meantime, if there's any new development give me a call, day or night, you have my contact details on your copy of the contract.'

Natalie stepped out of the shop and into a shower of icy rain. She needed to walk, it helped her think. Under the protection of a huge umbrella she set off. This wasn't going to be a simple case, but maybe if she could solve the mystery it would generate more clients. Taking early pension had seemed such a good idea at the time. She was glad to be away from the stress and responsibilities. But after taking an extended holiday and getting the house and garden in order, she'd had to admit, that she was mind numbingly bored. The agency had been her husband's idea, and she'd thrown herself and her money whole heartedly into it. But so far other than observing one philandering husband and a couple of light fingered part-timers, business had been slow.

She focused her mind to the case in hand. The best course of action she decided, would be to research into the Barringham family and their home. The building had been put to so many uses over the decades, perhaps there was a clue in that. She would need to delve into the background of the other two designers as well, and the fiancé, although she'd be surprised if the vet had much involvement. Grant Stevenson was a different kettle of fish. Everything revolved around his family, and the weird events seemed to coincide with his arrival. On the other hand, perhaps he'd trodden on someone's toes when he'd purchased the hall. He'd told her that he'd paid well over the asking price for it. She could check out who he'd outbid. It wouldn't be the first time that things had gone bump in the night and ghostly apparitions had mysteriously appeared, in an attempt to scare off the occupant and lower the property price. Although, on reflection, a ghost in a converted old hall would probably be good for business. Now there was another angle to consider.

The light from her house shone invitingly as Natalie parked the car and took a short cut across the lawn. Oh, good, John's home, she thought with a thrill of anticipation. She got to spend so little time with her detective husband that the prospect of an evening in front of the fire with him was delightful. A delicious aroma hit her as she opened the door. 'You're home early,' she called, hanging her coat in the cloakroom. She washed her hands, then made her way into the kitchen. John was standing at the cooker stirring the contents of a large pot. She noticed the expensive bottle of red wine breathing on the worktop, 'Well done, darling, you closed the case!' she said, wrapping her arms around his waist.

'Hey steady on, you'll get sauce all over the cooker,' he laughed, untangling himself. 'Go and pour yourself a glass of wine and put your feet up,' he said, playfully swatting her on the bottom with the tea-towel. 'Dinner will be ready in ten minutes.'

They ate their meal in companionable silence, then took their coffee through to the living room and Natalie told John how the interview with Lydia Lockwood had gone.

His reaction wasn't as cynical as she'd thought it might be. 'You know as well as I do,' he said, that the police have been known to use psychics in solving cases. But I agree, this does seem more like a hoax. Could it be a publicity stunt?'

'That was one of my theories, but they're well established and respected business people. They've asked me to keep the investigation confidential, so that theory seems weak. At least they've given me enough information to dig up some real facts. Have you ever heard of Barringham Hall, or rather the Meadow Bank Hall Hotel, as it's now known?'

'No, I've been called out to the housing estate a time or two, but I don't remember anything like an old hall or a hotel. I can ask around at the station, maybe some of the lads have turned out squatters over the years if the building's been derelict, or they might have had a meal at the hotel. Either way, right now, I'm looking forward to a night in with my gorgeous wife,' and he took the coffee cup out of her hands with an unmistakable gleam in his eyes.

Chapter Twenty-One

The meeting with Natalie Jacobs had taken longer than Grant had expected. It had also been more draining. He was feeling exhausted by the time he reached the hotel, but he still had his day's work to tackle. It was gone mid-night before he crawled into bed. The moment sleep came, another dream unfolded...

The young woman was concealed in the bushes bordering the station platform. Grant recognised her as the maid Polly. A lone soldier walked through the entrance, stiff backed, rigid with tension. Striding out, he'd covered the length of the platform in a few easy strides. Polly stepped cautiously from her hiding place, and seeing he was alone, ran to greet him.

Grant could hear a car approaching. It stopped out of sight, but the slamming of doors and angry voices seemed to alarm the pair. Smoothly the soldier pushed the girl into the nearest waiting room. Once inside he searched... for what? A hiding place? Then as though inspiration had struck he ushered her into the cubical of the gentleman's lavatory. He helped her climb up onto the seat to hold the door ajar with the hook while concealing her presence. Task complete, he was back on the platform just as two angry men entered the station.

The older of the pair, well to do, judging by the quality of his dinner suit, looked entirely at odds with the rustic setting. Eyes bulging, he thrust his puce face into the soldier's ashen one. Angry spittle showered the young soldiers face, but he didn't flinch.

The second man, possibly a gamekeeper, kept his head lowered…Embarrassed? Or subservient? Grant couldn't be sure. He was dressed in tweeds and Deerstalker hat, and carried a shot gun. It was loaded but broken and rested in the crook of his arm.

The altercation escalated between the older man and the soldier, until unexpectedly the man swung a punch at the soldier's jaw. He ducked and upper cut a full blow to the man's stomach.

'Shoot him,' the man gasped, 'Shoot the bloody young fool!'

The gamekeeper stood petrified to the spot.

'It's an order! I'm ordering you to shoot! You blasted oaf.'

Before the game-keeper could react, he'd snatched the shot-gun, snapped it together and fired at the soldier's abdomen. Blood spurted from the gaping wound splattering the man's face and staining his white shirt scarlet; red droplets, dripped from the starched collar.

Grant tossed and turned willing himself awake, desperate to escape the nightmare. He watched in horror as they carried the limp body away, then return; the gamekeeper to swill the platform, the man to search the perimeter. Looking for witnesses? Or was he after the young woman? He took a long time searching the Ladies waiting room, but to Grant's great relief, gave the Gentleman's only a cursory glance and left. The car engine fired up and gradually faded into the distance.

Moments later, the train rumbled into the station. Shielded by a cloud of steam, the young woman ran from her hiding place. She retrieved her suitcase from the shrubbery and leaped into a first-class carriage. Grant breathed a sigh of relief as the train pulled away…

In the morning on the dot of nine, Grant phoned Natalie Jacobs and gave her the details of the dream.

'As you already know,' he said, 'we suspect the soldier might be Frederick, the Barringham heir. I wanted to put you in the picture, in advance of you finding anything out about his death.'

'Wasn't he killed in France during the First World War?'

'According to the church records, yes.'

'But you think the dream was telling you otherwise?'

'I don't know about that. I'm just giving you the details. If I'd told you after you had presented the evidence you wouldn't have believed me, would you?'

'Alright, I've made a note, I'll add it to the investigation. If there's anything else you remember, call again.'

Natalie, sipped her coffee thinking if she counted every nightmare she'd had as a reality, she'd be a nervous wreck, particularly following the more gruesome cases she'd handled. Still she was getting paid to investigate the guy's fertile imagination, so investigate it she would. She picked up the phone and dialled the Reverend Byewaters. He confirmed Lydia's information on the Barringham family's history and then Natalie asked him if the church kept a log of parishioners.

'In those days? Yes of course, certainly of the regular worshippers.'

'Would that include a list of the servants working at Barringham Hall? I'm particularly interested in a lady's maid, called Polly, I need her surname. She probably attended church during the First World War, maybe towards the end.'

'I'd be happy to do that for you, but I will need a day or two, I'm rather busy with a run on funerals at present.'

'Would it be convenient for me to come over and look through the register myself? I'd like to get started on the case and I have a feeling this information is key to the investigation. I'm free this morning if that suits you?'

'Very well, shall we say about eleven, come to the vestry door at the side of the church? I'll leave the register on the desk.'

Natalie arrived early and had to wait respectfully at the lychgate, while a dear departed parishioner was conveyed ceremoniously down the path and into the church. Then she nipped down the side and into the vestry.

The last entry for Polly Brown in the register was for May 1917. There was no sign of the register for births, deaths and marriages, so Natalie unpacked her laptop and searched a genealogy website. She soon found Polly's details, she was a child at the time of the census, living with her family in the next village on from the hall.

Natalie took out her mobile and called Grant. 'Do you know what time of year it was in the scene at the station?'

'Spring, late spring. The buds were unfolding on the trees and there was blossom. No daffodils though.'

'Good, now I don't suppose you noticed where the train was going.'

'No, there was no announcement, it was early evening the place was deserted. There was nothing on the train to say.'

'Think, it's important. Sometimes they pin up notices on small country stations. Do you remember seeing anything? Was there a board? Take your time.'

The ticking of the clock on the vestry wall, punctuated the silence like a metronome as she waited. She had just drawn a breath to say not to worry, when he shouted 'Sandwich board! It was chalked up on a sandwich board. The next train through this station is at 19:00 hours in brackets 7 pm. Destination London. Why do you want to know?'

'I've got a hunch, I'll let you know if it's right,'

She scanned the church register again, it seemed that Polly's family had been regular attenders over the years, but there were no more entries for Polly. Why had she never returned home? Grant had said the man firing the gun hadn't seen her, so she shouldn't have been afraid... Then what would keep a young woman in 1917 away from her family? An illegitimate pregnancy? If she'd stayed in London where would she have gone? Taking a wild guess, Natalie typed in Frederick Brown born London around 1917. Hundreds of names popped up and she scrolled down methodically, until she found the most likely. Frederick Barringham Brown, born 14th February 1918. How sad, Natalie thought, to give birth to a dead lover's child on Valentine's Day. She had never felt the maternal urge, but her empathy for Polly was genuine. She clicked on information and discovered he'd been born in Kensington. Nice address.

The Reverend joined her then. 'That's a coincidence, I have an associate at a church in that area of London, would you like me to telephone him and ask if there is anything of interest in the church records?' Without waiting for a reply, he opened his phone book and tapped in the number.

After exchanging a few pleasantries with the person on the other end of the phone, he explained the reason for his call. 'I don't believe it!' he exclaimed moments later. 'How very strange, yes I'll wait.' He covered the mouth piece with his hand and turned to Natalie. 'Would you believe he has the register for the dates we need spread out on his desk? He had a telephone enquiry earlier in the week, the caller made an appointment for this morning but didn't show up. Hello, yes, I'm still here. You have? Right, yes, I understand, thank you for your help. No problem, I will. Goodbye.'

'Did he find anything useful?'

'Indeed, he did. Sad news I'm afraid. Polly gave birth to the baby in the workhouse in that parish. The building took a bit of a bashing during the Second World War apparently; however, the records survived and were eventually transferred to the workhouse archives. He is sending me further details via email. It shouldn't take too long.'

'I'm very grateful for your help,' Natalie said. 'Do you know which regiment Frederick belonged to?'

'Yes, you'll find the details on the memorial plaque in the church. There's an hour before the next funeral, so you've time to go through and get the information. I'm going to put the kettle on would you like a drink?'

'Tea please, milk no sugar, thank you.'

Natalie eyed the war memorial and wondered why so little had been made of Frederick's death, he was after all the heir of the local gentry and yet his name was in amongst the list of local lads. It's not as though he was of the same regiment, she thought.

She voiced her thoughts to the Reverend Byewaters over their cup of tea.

'I understand what you mean, but so many young men from the village lost their lives. Perhaps the family didn't want to give the impression their son's life was more important than the rest.'

'What, in an era when people were taught that the gentry were their betters, I hardly think so.'

'I'll check if that email has arrived,' the Reverend said, setting down his tea cup. Clearly ending any further discussion on class distinction.

John Jacobs, was owed some leave. And so, the following week, when Natalie made the trip to London, he went along. 'I'll be surprised if the workhouse records reveal much, if the baby's birth certificate stated father unknown.'

'I know, you're probably right. In those days, the authorities always put father unknown when the mother was unmarried, that doesn't rule out Frederick being the father. What I'm trying to prove is whether the facts back up what my clients are telling me. I'm hoping I might find a more structured report about Frederick's army service and the details of how he died. That should put paid to Grant Stevenson's claim that some lunatic shot him on a deserted station.'

At the archive office, the clerk had prepared the documentation on Polly in advance of their arrival.

'It was no trouble at all, glad to oblige,' she said, 'Anything else I can help you with just give me a shout, I'm in the next room along.'

The workhouse admissions record showed that Polly had worked in a public house as a skivvy up until the time she'd entered the workhouse, only days before the baby's birth.

'Her last given address was the same as the pubs, presumably she was a live-in skivvy.'

'It was probably the best job she could find without a reference. She'll have gone into the workhouse to have the baby because she couldn't afford to pay medical expenses.'

'Where else could she have gone? I expect the landlord only put up with her condition so long as she could work.'

Natalie flicked through the pages of the ledger until she found where the baby's birth was recorded. There was a book mark poking out further along the ledger and she turned the pages back.

John was the first to spot a discharge entry for Polly. 'She found herself a job as a house-keeper.'

'A house keeper to Myles Barringham? Now that's curious. My clients believe the baby's father was Frederick, and that's the name she christened him. Although Reverend Byewaters has a suspicion that the baby might have been Myles' based on his reputation as the black sheep of the family. A reputation he'd earned, even before he'd absconded with the family jewels. Grant Stevenson denied the rumour about the jewels, but it makes you wonder whether Myles was the father after all.'

'There's no mention of the baby being discharged with her. I know children were separated from their mothers. I'm not sure how young though.'

'I noticed that, I'll go and ask.'

The clerk came back into the room with Natalie. She lifted another ledger from the shelf and placed it on the table then she deftly flicked through it with an experienced eye. 'Ah, there you go. There was an outbreak of diphtheria in the workhouse, the healthy infants were taken to an orphanage.' She leafed through the pages of another ledger to find what she was after and a smile lit up her face. 'There,' she said, clearly delighted. 'Frederick Barringham Brown, aged 10

182

months, discharged into the care of the birth mother. She took him with her when she left with Myles Barringham. The child has the same name. Is there a family connection?'

'That's part of our investigation,' Natalie said, 'But yes there's a strong possibility.'

Outside the archive building. The smell of fresh coffee drew them towards a cafe. There, they ordered Mediterranean Paninis and coffee. 'What do you make of the case so far, John said, biting into the Panini.

'Well, we've confirmed that Polly caught the London train. We've also found a connection to the Barringham name. But the information was there to be found. How would we know whether someone's already looked it up and used it to scare the wits out of Lydia Lockwood? The Reverend Byewaters told me that someone had made an appointment to look in the Kensington parish records but they hadn't kept the appointment. That person could be on the same trail as me and I don't see how I can find out what their purpose is. As yet, I'm no nearer to finding out why anyone would want to frighten Lydia and try to make her believe she's going insane. Neither does it confirm that she or Grant have a psychic link with the past.'

The search for Frederick's war record, proved to be fruitless. They were told that the records had been destroyed in a fire during the First World War.

As the train pulled out of the station, Natalie said, 'Am I being cynical John, or do you think it's a coincidence that the records were destroyed in a fire.'

'I don't know love, there was such carnage at that point in the war they lost trace of the people never mind their records. It could have been as simple as a cigarette left burning.'

'Yes, I suppose you're right,' she said, but something niggled at the back of her mind, the seed of an idea, she just couldn't quite grasp it.

Chapter Twenty-Two

Under the helm of a different architect, the hotel's transformation from minimalist to Art Deco, was completed with a speed that left even Grant astounded. Corners hadn't been cut either, the craftsmanship was excellent. Much of the speed was down to organisation and timing. That wasn't entirely due to the architect, it was more to do with Jenny's impeccable organisation skills. The way she had overseen and managed the project was faultless and Grant wondered what it would take to temp her away from Deco Designs.

It had been a winter without snow, nevertheless it had been long and hard, even for the North of England. Despite that, or perhaps because of it, April burst into spring seemingly overnight. The sun shone warmly for the whole month, and the occasional shower of gentle rain painted rainbows across a vivid blue sky. The flowers, escaping their buds at last, opened their petals and lifted their faces to the sun.

The morning of the garden party found Grant patrolling the grounds making last minute checks. Vintage cars lined the driveway and he stopped to chat to some of the drivers as they polished already gleaming paintwork and tied ribbons and flowers to the wedding cars, in one case, a string of tin cans and old boots. From her vantage point at the head of the steps, Lydia searched for Myles distinctive car, despising herself for doing so. She turned and walked through the hotel and onto the terrace. Down in the garden, the waiting staff were buzzing about near the tents. They looked smart, dressed in traditional black and white. In contrast, the Jazz band added a splash of colour, with their green and yellow striped waist coats and matching bow ties.

As the visitors began to filter through to the gardens, Lydia was pleased to see that the majority had made the effort to come in vintage clothes. She recognised several of her creations. The refreshment tent was soon full and a long queue had formed outside. She managed to sneak a cream tea from the tray of a passing waitress. She hadn't had time for breakfast and she was ravenous.

The band struck up a Charleston, and attracted by the music she wandered over to where a local dance school were performing. She applauded loudly, smiling and nodding her congratulations to the young performers as they made their exit. Then the band leader invited the spectators to have a go. She felt a tug at her elbow and turned to see Myles. 'Come on old bean,' he smiled, 'Let's show them how it's done.' She ran on to the dance floor, bursting with happiness and the sheer joy of being with him. The spectators cheered them on and they soon found themselves dancing alone in the centre of the floor to thunderous applause. At the end, they bowed dramatically and hand in hand made their escape across the lawn.

Myles guided her into a secluded walled garden she hadn't come across before.

'I'm not dreaming this, am I?' she gasped, trying to catch her breath. 'You were dancing with me in the present time.' He didn't answer, instead he pulled her into his arms and kissed her, and any logical question she was about to ask dissolved.

'Come on,' he said, 'let's see if I've still got the knack,' and taking her hand he pulled her round the side of the building. Instantly everything familiar slipped once again into the unfamiliar. Where the walls had been bare and the stone work smooth, there now grew shrubs and bushes. Trained wisteria and honeysuckle covered the walls outlining windows, which Lydia knew only existed on the original plans.

'You have to explain,' she pleaded, 'Tell me what's happening.'

'Later,' he said, giving her hand a squeeze,

'What are you doing?' she asked, watching him jab his hand into the bushes every so often working his way up the wall.

'Quiet, I'm counting,' he said. He stopped jabbing at shoulder height and began to work his way across to the right. 'Got it!' he shouted triumphantly. Lydia heard a click and then the scraping sound of stone and metal as a section of the wall miraculously moved towards her. Myles stepped inside and ran his hand along a high ledge above the door. He struck a match and she watched as a small flame inside a hurricane lamp burst into life.

He held his hand out, 'Come inside, will you? This is supposed to be a secret entrance. With you standing there in your red dress, the rest of the garden party will be joining us any minute now.' She stepped into the opening beside him and the mechanism sealed shut the entrance behind her.

'This leads to my brother's suite of rooms,' he said. She had expected the passageway to be damp and musty and full of cobwebs, but it was fresh and recently swept.

'We discovered this as teenagers,' he explained. 'It came in jolly handy a time or two I can tell you. I don't imagine our parents knew of its existence, given the state it was in.'

They emerged into a room completely at odds with Myles suite. A dark oak, four poster bed dominated the room. Brocade drapes, in a rich burgundy, were tied back either side of the bed head and a matching plump eiderdown covered the mattress.

The clock over the fireplace chimed four. Mesmerised by the hypnotic swing of the pendulum, Lydia wondered how one measured time, since time was a diverse relativity. Four o'clock on a Saturday in May...But in which decade?

'Tea, that's what we need. A strong cup of tea,' he said, pressing a button on the wall beside the fireplace. His leg brushed against the fresh lilies in the hearth sending a cloud of perfume into the room and smudging pollen on the knee of his white flannels. 'We won't be disturbed in here,' he said, pulling up a chair for her and placing it beside an occasional table. 'I'll just get another chair.'

Left alone, Lydia surveyed the room. Dominating the far wall was a huge, ornately carved ebony wardrobe. At the corner of the room was a sink and a marble wash stand, where a gentleman's toilette was neatly laid out. Light flooded into the room from the floor to ceiling bay window, its central door opened onto a small balcony. With a start, Lydia realised this was the room Grant used as his living room. Myles returned just then, carrying a chair followed soon afterwards by a maid carrying a tray of tea. She put it down on the table beside Lydia and left the room.

'I'm sorry, I know I owe you an explanation,' he said, sitting down, 'but it's complicated and I'm dashed if I know where to begin.' He reached across the table for her hand, 'Lydia, do you remember there's an afterlife?' his steady blue gaze searched her eyes.

'Remember?'

'Believe then,' he sighed, releasing her hand. He stood up and walked over to the fireplace running a hand distractedly through his hair. He turned to face her and opened his mouth as though to speak and closed it again. Instead he paced back and forth across the fireplace.

'You're never going to get the stains out of those trousers if you keep that up,' she said.

'What? Oh, I see,' and he brushed the brown lily pollen off his flannels. 'I say, are you ever going to pour that tea? I'm parched.'

So much for the suffragette movement, she thought, reaching for the tea pot. 'How do you want it, milk or lemon?'

She let him finish his tea, then she said, 'I know I'm not dreaming, so am I time travelling or are you a ghost, or some sort of spirit?'

'Some would call me that. I have simply moved on to the next dimension.'

'So you can cross back and forth between dimensions?'

'Not usually, only when exceptional circumstances coincide with a perfect alignment between the planets and the celestial planes... Do you remember the stifling humidity before the electrical storms? Those weather conditions were caused by the planets aligning. Was the sky covered with stars?'

'Yes, I ...'

'You made a wish, I know, your voice guided me.'

'You know what I wished for?'

'It was an integral part in the greater scheme. What was it you said, a gallant English gentleman, to whisk you away to some other time and place? A pretty spot on description of me I should say.'

Embarrassed, she ignored his comment, instead she said, 'After I made the wish, I went into the shop, the atmosphere had changed. I sensed something. I saw something, shadows. There were shadows just beyond the moonlight.'

'There are many forces that I don't understand. Such an alignment upsets much of the cosmic levels.'

'Where are we now? How do I travel so easily into the past?'

'You're seeing a place just beyond reach of most mortals. Where souls wait, earthbound, mostly by choice, for release into the next dimension.'

'But how am I here?'

'As I said, such a strong cosmic formation causes all sorts of disruption. Your wish was key to my success in crossing the parallels and it awakened a psychic energy in you.'

'If you'd already moved on to the next dimension, what are you doing here?'

'Something happened during my last lifetime on earth that really wasn't my fault and I couldn't have prevented it. When I discovered the truth, I did my best to repair the damage. It wasn't enough. And because of what happened, the people I most want to spend eternity with can't be together. That's why I came through to earth's dimension to try and amend the wrong doing. I've been allowed to come back for that purpose only. I've waited decades for a suitable planetary alignment. You were chosen as my guide, and Grant as the instigator, in helping me resolve the problem.'

'A Lady Barringham came into my shop.'

'Yes, it's one of her favourite places. She's visited many times. The day that you saw her, was when she realised that my return had awoken your psychic ability.'

'What was all that fuss about with the dress?'

'Oh, that's just her wicked sense of humour. She chose the dress for you to wear to the Midsummer's Eve ball. She wanted you to look pretty, as a surprise for me. It was a surprise alright. I couldn't understand what you were doing there, I had no idea you would be able to see me. I nearly tumbled down the staircase with you when I found you standing there.'

'But isn't she your wife? What kind of wife, would want another woman, to look pretty for her husband?'

'Yes, she was my wife during our lifetime, but now...' he ran his hands through his hair again. 'Look here, there's a jolly good reason why she did it. Can't you leave it at that? Damn and blast it all Lydia. It should have been so simple. A jolly trip back to earth, sort out the blithering mess we made of it the first time around and Bob's your uncle, everything's as it should be and we all exist happily ever after. I'd quite forgotten how human emotions mess things up!'

'I'm sorry, are you blaming my emotions for something?'

'No, mine. And that's something else I can't explain.'

'So what about Grant? Is he psychic too?'

'No. I can reach him through dreams.'

'Ah the dreaded dreams. Was it you who sent him the email about the hall?'

'My energy yes.'

'What is it you want from us Myles? How can we help you, if you won't tell us?'

'I can't give you any more information, it will ruin everything. All I can say is listen to Natalie Jacobs. I know you haven't been impressed by her so far, but she's on the right track. You'll discover what I'm doing here soon enough.'

She got up and walked over to the bay window. She was surprised to see the day had turned dull. Dark clouds were gathering on the horizon and people scattered as the first rumble of thunder rolled over the valley. She opened the French doors and stepped onto the balcony for a better look. The scene playing out on the lawn below could have belonged to the twentieth century, but she recognised it for what it was, a fancy-dress garden party in the twenty-first century. 'How can I be sure any of this is real? How do I know that I'm not completely insane?'

'Do you remember dancing in the moonlight on the terrace Lydia,' he said, coming to stand behind her. 'Do you recall I asked you then, if you believed in shooting stars and magic? You still haven't given me your answer... Trust in me Lydia, and trust Grant, he's a decent fellow. You know he's falling in love with you.'

She turned to face him, 'I believe in wishes on shooting stars, I believe in magic and... I believe I'm falling in love with you.' She saw a look of doubt in his eyes, a moment's hesitation and then he was kissing her, greedy hungry kisses. The heat of his body burned into her flesh igniting an inner fire as the first flash of lightening illuminated the sky and thunder exploded overhead shaking the balcony beneath their feet. Bodies entwined, mouths exploring greedily, the rain splattered down all around them, great fat globules exploding on impact. Her hair was plastered to her head, her dress sodden and clinging. All the time as though in competition with the elements, his kisses rained down on her face, her neck her breasts as fiercely as the torrential rain.

When he took her hand, and guided her towards the four-poster bed; she could not have resisted him, had her life depended upon it. He lay with her, his muscular body pinning her to the bed, burning her with desire. Her last conscious thought, before floating away on a sea of ecstasy, was that it didn't matter that she was giving herself to this man, it was only a dream, a fantasy that couldn't harm her.

She woke with a start, she was lying in the middle of Grant's living room floor, her clothes scattered about. She jumped up as she heard the door unlocking. Gathering her things, she ran into the bathroom and switched on the shower. 'Hi,' she called, 'I hope you don't mind, I got caught in the downpour.'

She stayed under the hot shower longer than was necessary to gather her thoughts. She eventually emerged with her hair wrapped up turban style and a bath sheet wrapped around her body.

Grant was standing with his back to the fireplace in the living room. 'Hi, how you doing?' he said.

She couldn't miss the glint in his eye and she felt her cheeks redden. 'I just came through to collect my bag. I brought jeans and a top to change into after the garden party.' He handed her the bag and she disappeared into the bathroom. She dragged a brush through her tangle of hair, marvelling at how straight it looked when wet, and yet in a few moments tendrils would appear around her face until her whole head was a mass of curls. She didn't mind the curls: it was the frizz she objected to. Her blonde eyelashes made her eyes look childlike. Without make up she looked younger than her twenty-seven years, but she was tired and couldn't be bothered with make-up. She finger-pressed her hair into some semblance of shape and went through to the living room.

'Tea or wine?' Grant said, holding up a bottle.

'Tea please, it'll warm me up and… and … I have to drive home.' The words caught in her throat and her stomach squirmed with embarrassment at the sight of Myles portrait. She was unsure whether the afternoon spent with him had been a hallucination or not.

'Grant raised an eyebrow. I thought we'd arranged that you stay over? I've ordered dinner.'

'Dinner would be nice, but I have to get back. The dog minder can't keep Billy overnight, she has an early appointment.' The excuse sounded lame, but Grant didn't pull her up on it. He seemed preoccupied with the portrait of Lady Barringham, 'You know,' he said, 'I've been staring at this portrait for days now, wracking my brains trying to remember where else I've seen that same face and those violet eyes. It's just come to me now, if the hair was longer, she'd be the image of the maid Polly.'

'Perhaps you dreamed the maid had that same face, because you'd already seen it in the portrait.'

'Yeah, I guess you're right.'

Chapter Twenty-Three

Natalie Jacobs had resorted to bribery. She had placed an advertisement in the local papers offering a reward for information about the late Myles and Frederick Barringham, of Barringham Hall. Now known as the Meadow Bank Hall Hotel. She had painstakingly sorted through letters from the fraudulent, avaricious and deluded respondents, until finally she had come across one that evoked a little ray of hope. The letter was from a woman claiming to be the gamekeeper's granddaughter and Natalie had made an appointment to interview her. The woman's bungalow stood in a generous plot with a crazy paving path meandering to a bright red door. Either side of the path, a profusion of plants vied for space in an explosion of colour. Natalie pushed open the gate and stepped through just in time to avoid being hit by it, as an overzealous spring, snapped it shut again. Instantly the red door flew open and there stood a short, stout woman with an ample bosom and a cheerful grin. 'Gives a better warning than any watchdog that gate does,' she chuckled.

'Hello there... Mrs. Marsh?' Natalie ventured.

'That's right love, but call me Beryl and you must be Natalie Jacobs. Come on in love, I've got the kettle on.' She ushered Natalie into a cosy farmhouse style kitchen where a range omitted warmth and a delicious smell of baking. It was welcoming on such a cool blustery day. 'I'll just take those scones out before they catch, then I'll make us a nice cup of tea. Sit yourself down love,' Beryl said, pulling out a pine chair from under the well-scrubbed table.

Pleasantries over and tea and scones served, Beryl got straight down to business. 'There's something that troubled my mam the rest of her days, she didn't know what to do for the best see. She thought it was just an old man's ramblings on his death bed. He told her something, that he'd never been able to tell a living soul. Too dangerous for his family he said, they'd have been evicted. And he was scared for himself as well. Scared they'd have him put away in the prison or the asylum. My mam told him to hush; no one was going to put him away. Then he became right agitated like. He grabbed mam's wrist and told her straight. 'You got to tell 'em the truth, Mary lass. You can tell the whole world for all I care. They can't touch me now. I'm for the next world anytime, and they can't hurt you.... Not now any road. Only knee high to a grass hopper you were at the time. Promise me lass, that when I'm gone, you'll tell them authorities. When the truth's out the lad's soul can rest in peace... and so shall mine.' Them's his exact words.'

'Do you know what it was your mother was supposed to tell the authorities?'

'Oh yes, it was his dying words.'

Natalie waited with baited breath for Beryl to reveal the dying man's words, but Beryl had a question for her. 'You are a retired police detective, right? Well what I want to know, before I tell you what he said, is whether me and my family could be in any kind of danger from them descendants of the Barringham family or from the police for that matter?'

'Well you'd have to tell me what it was about before I could answer that, but I can't see there being a problem. You can't be held responsible for something that your grandfather was involved in.'

'Even if I was reporting a murder?' Beryl persisted. Natalie was sitting on the edge of her seat. It was taking all her reserve not to scream at the woman. 'Just tell me what he said.'

'Well you see, my mam never did tell the authorities, she took the secret to the grave with her.'

'What!' Natalie exploded, 'You mean you don't know what he told her?' Natalie could hear the shriek in her voice and fought to gain control of the little patience she had left.

'Of course she told me,' Beryl said, flapping her hand at Natalie's impatience. 'She told me... she just never told no authorities.'

After clarifying that point, Beryl seemed to drift off into a world of her own.

'And,' Natalie prompted.

'Oh, sorry... Yes, he told her that the Master ordered him to shoot young Master Frederick.'

'So, Frederick wasn't killed in the First World War as everyone had been led to believe. He was shot by your grandfather?'

'No, no. You've got it all wrong, my grandad was ordered to shoot him, but when he didn't, the Master grabbed his gun and he shot Frederick.'

'Wait a minute, let me get this straight. You're saying that Lord Barringham shot his own son, his heir. Do you know why?'

'Of course I do. He was eloping with one of the maids. Polly her name was. Grandad overheard her telling her brother all about it. He was one of the grooms see, and grandad heard them discussing it in the stables. Anyway, he decided it was a ploy on Frederick's part to have his wicked way with her. So, he went to tell Lord Barringham, thinking he would put a stop to it before Polly got herself into trouble. He'd no idea anything like that would happen. He'd known the Master had a temper on him, but murder? No, he'd not been prepared for that.'

As Natalie sat and listened to the rest of the tale an icy tingle crept up her spine. It was an exact recount of Grant's dream.

'Would you like another cuppa love? You've gone awfully white,' Beryl said, getting to her feet.

'No, I'll be fine, honestly. You've been very helpful, thank you.'

'It's a relief to get it off my chest to be honest. Did the advertisement say anything about a reward?' Beryl looked down at her expectantly.

'It did indeed,' Natalie said, and she handed over a thin wad of crisp notes. Beryl tucked them safely inside her apron pocket. 'Much obliged,' she said, patting the pocket. 'If there's anything else I can assist you with, please call again.'

'I'll be sure to, oh there is one other thing I'm curious about. How long have you known Grant Stevenson?'

'Grant who?'

'Stevenson.'

'No, can't say I've ever heard of him. Is he a local lad?'

Natalie was smirking to herself as she climbed into her car. Decades of keeping a family secret, broken by the promise of a golden handshake. She didn't blame Beryl; it was never her secret to keep. Her grandfather though, well, it would have been quite a different story for him. If the truth about Frederick's death had got out, it would have meant certain ruin. It could even have meant death. Lord Barringham had been a magistrate, that much Natalie had discovered. He could have pinned the crime on the gamekeeper or continued with the war injury charade and had him committed to an asylum as a madman. Either way as gamekeeper, his house would have been tied to the job and his family would have been evicted. 'Oh, dammit,' Natalie cursed. 'I forgot to ask what happened to Frederick's body.' She climbed out of the car and mindful of the gate this time, retraced her steps. Beryl Marsh was waiting at the door.

'What happened to Frederick?' Natalie said.

'Thought you'd be back, missed out the most important bit.'

The cunning old battle axe, thought Natalie, she's after another few quid.

'Well,' Beryl said, stretching her story out as far as she could. 'They got him back to the hall and sent for the village doctor, but it was too late. Frederick was already dead.'

'What did they do with the body?'

'They put it in the family crypt in the grounds. My mam said fancy going through all that pomp and ceremony supposedly bringing his body back from France. It must have been an empty coffin. Either that or they brought some other beggar back. There'd be enough of the poor souls lying around to choose from by all accounts.'

Driving home, Natalie wondered how the hell Lord Barringham had managed to pull it all off, let alone get away with it? Even accounting for the fact that he was a Lord, and a magistrate, at a time when the upper classes ruled; surely, he would have had trouble bribing a doctor and the military into covering up a murder. She would need to dig deeper into Lord Barringham's history. Perhaps she should start with his army records. Family tradition probably dictated that Frederick joined the same Regiment as his father. She would begin her search there.

As soon as she reached home she phoned Grant Stevenson. 'Have you ever met a Beryl Marsh?'

'No, I don't think so. Why?'

'Just curious. You remember the gamekeeper in your dream? Beryl Marsh is his grandaughter. I interviewed her today. She gave me an accurate recount of your dream. It would appear, that you were dreaming about a real historical event. Mr Stevenson... Grant, are you being straight with me, are you giving me all the facts? I don't appreciate being made to look a fool. If you're hiding something, I'd rather you told me now.'

'Why would I bring you on board if I had something to hide? In any case, most of the weird stuff is happening to Lydia not me.'

'That's precisely my point. Things only started happening after you bought the hall. Believe me, I'm a far better detective than you seem to be giving me credit for. I will find out the truth,' and she disconnected the call.

Lydia's mobile rang. It was Grant, she didn't answer. He'd phoned all day Sunday, but she needed time and space, she couldn't get her head around what Myles had said, let alone what had happened. She blushed at the thought. How could it have been an illusion? Yet the reality was impossible to believe.

Monday was a beautiful day, she'd promised to help Pippa with the final fitting of her bridal gown, but there was plenty of time for a walk first. She needed to get up onto the moors and blow away the cobwebs. She always returned refreshed and clear minded.

Half an hour later she was striding along the path looking down on Hathersage in the distance. Up here she felt on top of the world. The wind flapped her clothes as though at any moment it might pick her up and set her down in the village. She marched on through the gorse and bracken heading for the rock formation at the summit, the exertion banishing the tension. She scrambled over the rocks and stood surveying the panoramic view. It was like standing on the rim of a giant bowl lined with gorse and heather leading down to a lush patchwork of emerald green, its squares separated by dry stone walls and speckled with sheep and cattle. A hamlet of white houses nestled in the basin, wood smoke curled lazily from an occasional chimney. The river Derwent meandered like a glittering ribbon in the distance. She imagined the villager's in their houses, busily getting on with their lives. Had anyone of them ever experienced what she was going through? Was there even one other person in the whole world who'd shared her experience. She didn't want to think about it just now, this was her happy place, and yet she couldn't shake off the niggling doubt that there was no hoax being played; she was simply losing her sanity.

In the distance, she could see a loan figure striding purposefully along, head bend against the wind. She dropped down out of sight. She wasn't in the mood for company. She took out a flask of coffee from her ruck-sack and poured herself a cup. Then she leaned back against a rock surveying the view and waiting for the feeling of contentment to unfold as it always did in this place.

'Hi,' Grant said, startling her as he dropped down beside her. 'Have I done something to offend you?'

'No, you haven't offended me,' she said, moving over to make room for him. 'Life seems to be overwhelming right now, that's all.'

'Are you overwhelmed by fact or fiction?' he asked. She thought about it for a few moments, unsure how to answer. 'Fact, beyond comprehension,' she sighed. 'How did you know where to find me?'

'Telepathy.'

'Stop it, I don't even want to joke about it.'

'I phoned the shop, Pippa told me you'd gone for a walk on the moors. Then I phoned your dog minder to see if she knew where you were most likely to be up here with a dog. The reason I've been trying to contact you all weekend, is because I had a call from Natalie Jacobs. She found the gamekeeper. The one from my dream. Well not him, but his grandaughter. Her story was an exact recount of the one I told you and Natalie. I guess that means I was dreaming about a real event. The trouble is, now Natalie thinks I'm the hoaxer targeting you. Do you think that?'

'You know I did, in the beginning. That's why I came to see you. Now it seems to me we're in this together. Come on,' she said, 'let's walk back, I need to tell you something. I didn't want to, but now... I think I need to.'

Pippa was locking up by the time Lydia got back to the shop. 'Right on time,' she said, the dress is out ready, and the kettle has just boiled if you want a cuppa first.'

'Fantastic, I'll just get Billy settled and change out of these jeans, they're a bit muddy.'
The dress was waiting on a tailor's dummy. Pippa lifted it off and slipped it over her head. The oyster satin slipped easily over her body, the soft folds settling in a subtle, yet most flattering way, accenting her natural curves. It tapered in slightly below the knee leaving the hemline to pool into a

small train at the back. The colour was warming, making Pippa's olive skin glow. The soft folds of the cowl neck draped gently over her bosom at the front and dropped dramatically at the back creating the appearance of height and slender. Pippa had worked hard creating the look she desired.

'Breath-taking,' Lydia exclaimed, standing back and admiring the work of art, 'you don't really need my help,' she said, lifting the cowl to check the darts were sitting nicely, 'you've done it all yourself. You look truly beautiful.' Pippa flushed with pleasure.

'Something borrowed,' Lydia suddenly remembered, and dashed out of the workroom. She returned a few minutes later with the shooting star brooch. 'Here,' she said, holding it against Pippa's left shoulder, 'you see, it sits perfectly with the style of the dress, and after all, it was the wish on a shooting star that made your dreams come true,' she smiled, giving Pippa's arm a squeeze.

Later that evening Natalie Jacobs telephoned Grant, 'We'll need to confirm Beryl Marsh's information. Do I have your permission to set the wheels in motion to open the crypt? If they find a likely body, they can check the DNA although it's going to have to be specific. Presumably all the occupants are your ancestors. I doubt that there will be any dental records but if there's anything left of the uniform they'll check that out. The buttons should be intact.'

The following week, with Grant having given his permission for Natalie to proceed, Jenny and Lydia called on Reverend Byewaters to ask him to say a prayer when Frederick's body was exhumed and hold a befitting service when it was interned again. The housekeeper had shown them into the library and brought them a tea tray. The Reverend was frantically searching through papers on the desk. 'Oh dear, oh dear, I'm afraid I'm in rather a muddle,' he said. 'I've double booked a wedding and I can't find the relevant paperwork. I know I had it out on the desk yesterday afternoon.'

Lydia could see an A4 diary on the floor. It had fallen between the paper basket and the side of the desk. She bent to pick it up. As she handed it over, some papers fell out onto the desk.

'Oh, thank heavens you arrived when you did,' he exclaimed, pouncing on the papers and giving them a cursory glance. 'I'll just make a couple of urgent phone calls and then you shall have my undivided attention.'

Lydia ran a hand along the top of the desk. 'This is late Edwardian, an exquisite piece of furniture.'

'I noticed it as soon as we walked into the room.' Jenny said, 'I wonder if he realises what a rare piece it is.'

'Possibly, I'll quiz him about it when he comes back. It would look perfect in the shop instead of the counter. Do you think I dare make him an offer for it? Or is that too cheeky?'

'Problem solved,' the Reverend said, coming back into the room. 'Now what can I do for you?'

They explained why they'd called to see him and he offered some helpful advice, as well as explaining the logistics. When they were leaving, Lydia mentioned the quality of the desk.

'I suppose it is an attractive piece, yes. It was donated to the vicarage when the Doctor's surgery was replaced by the medical centre. Is it valuable do you think? We're desperate to raise money to repair the church roof?'

'Yes, it's quite a rare piece,' she said, and told him what a collector would be likely to pay for it. She couldn't help smiling at his shocked expression.

'Goodness, I'm indebted to you twice in one day,' he said. 'First you find the missing paperwork and now you've solved the problem of funding repairs to the church roof. Do you know anyone who might be interested in buying the desk?'

'Yes, me,' she laughed. 'Please feel free to check that the price I've suggested is the going rate, but you can be sure I'm pretty up-to-date on these things.'

'I am in no doubt about that at all,' he said, reaching across the desk and shaking her hand, 'We have a deal.'

'Great, I'll be in touch to arrange collection. I'll probably get a French Polisher to pick it up. I've noticed a few chips and scratches.'

Thrilled with her purchase, Lydia's spirits should have been high as they drove to their next appointment. Her excitement was overshadowed by the apprehension she was feeling about her riding lesson, later that afternoon.

'Bagged yourself a bargain there,' Jenny said. I thought you'd be jumping for joy, what's up?'

'He's done alright out of it. He wouldn't have got that at auction. I've just cut out the middle man. I'm thrilled, really. It's just… Well I'm a bit nervous about the riding lesson this afternoon. You and Grant are accomplished riders. I'm going to feel like an overgrown school kid plodding around the ménage while you too gallop off into the sunset.'

'Everyone's got to learn, and we might be galloping off into the sunset, but not in the way you mean. He only has eyes for you.'

'Really? Well he might have changed his mind since I told him about the romantic interlude with Myles Barringham.'

'I thought you weren't going to tell him?'

'I wasn't, but after Beryl Marsh's story matched so closely to Grant's dream, Natalie Jacobs thinks he's the one pulling some sort of hoax or scam on me. I know that's what I thought in the beginning, but not now. You believe Grant is genuine, don't you?'

'Well, if I don't, we're back to square one with the why and how, and really I should say he's got much more to lose than us if his credibility takes a beating. He'd be big news both sides of the Atlantic.'

'Anyway, I told him because as much as anything I wanted his opinion on all this afterlife and parallel worlds stuff. I wish I'd left the romantic bit out though. It just sort of blended in with the rest of the story and before I knew it I couldn't stop. He didn't seem to take it too well, although he didn't actually say very much.'

'We're here,' Jenny said, pulling into the kerb, 'the white house on the corner.'

'The one with the awful imitation gas lamp in the garden?'

Several weeks had gone by since that first riding lesson. Lydia had surprised herself with how well she had taken to the saddle. She hadn't divulged the fact that she had ridden as a child even to Jenny, just in case she'd made a complete hash of it as an adult. She'd progressed so well that the instructor felt confident enough to take her through some practice jumps. She was pleased because it meant she was another step closer to Grant. Riding was a big part of his life, particularly in America. Myles hadn't put in an appearance since the garden party and she and Grant had been getting along like a house on fire; socially as well as in business. It had surprised her, how jealous she felt about the close friendship he had with Jenny. It had developed during the time it had taken to refurbish the hotel and their discovery of a mutual love of horse riding.

'Don't worry about the jumps,' the instructor was saying, 'we'll start with the posts on the ground for the horse to step over and gradually build up the jumps as your confidence and technique improves.' Lydia put her horse through the warm up practice, starting and stopping, changing direction trotting and cantering. Seeing Jenny and Grant walk their horses out of the yard together made her heart constrict, but she smiled and waved. They walked over to join her in the ménage. Jack, her instructor, had decided it would be good practice for her to work the space with other horses and together they went through the warm up routine again. They had begun to build up to the jumps when Grant glanced at his watch and said, 'I've got to be heading back in another half hour, just time for a gallop to the top field and back, you coming Jenny or are you staying here?'

'Your horse could do with a good gallop,' Jack told her, 'this is the first time he's been out today.' When Grant and Jenny turned their horses around and jumped the low boundary of the ménage, Lydia's horse made to follow. She sat back hard in the saddle and pulled on the reins but the horse had the bit between its teeth. It wanted to be free up on the hills and took off after the galloping horses. She held her seat gripping with her knees as the ground sped by beneath her, and the wind rushed passed her cheeks. Exhilarated, she urged the horse on to catch up with Jenny and Grant. Her lack of experience gave her no warning of the impending danger as she hurled towards hedges twice the height of the practice enclosure. She was almost upon the first hedge before she realised and then panic rendered her useless.

Suddenly out of the corner of her eye, she saw a rider fast approaching from the right. At the last possible moment before her horse prepared for flight, the rider grabbed the reins and still galloping used his horse to force hers away from the hedge.

Grant, she thought, thank goodness, he must have seen the horse bolt. They galloped together down the field towards the ménage, slowing to a canter. She felt back in control now and slowed her horse to a trot. As her breathing steadied she looked around to thank Grant, but horse and rider were nowhere to be seen. Before she could ponder their disappearance, two riders cantered out of the stable block towards her. One of them she recognised as Jack her instructor.

When he was close enough, he drew his horse alongside hers and grabbed the reins, 'What just happened, are you ok?'

'Fine, thanks to Grant, but I don't know where he's disappeared to.'

'That wasn't Grant, he and Jenny are way over on the top field.'

'Then who came to my rescue? He looked exactly like...Myles,' she gasped.

'Well, I don't know any Myles, but he can certainly handle a horse. I know I couldn't have controlled the situation as easily as he did.' Jack was full of admiration for the rider and apologies that the horse had bolted in the first place. 'I hope it hasn't put you off riding, you're a natural.'

'Not at all, it was exhilarating until I realised the height of the hedge and that the horse was going to jump it.'

They walked their horses back to the stables and dismounted. Lydia could see Jenny and Grant cantering down the field towards her. On the horizon behind them, a lone rider stood in the saddle and raised his hat in salute. She touched her fingers to her lips and held them aloft. Reining in his horse, he turned and galloped hard towards the high hedge, cleared it easily and disappeared once more from her life.

Chapter Twenty-Four

'Penny for them?' Pippa said, placing a cup of tea in front of Lydia.

Raising a smile, Lydia thanked her, 'Sorry, I can't stop thinking about Natalie Jacobs' phone call. What an evil man that old Lord Barringham was. This must be what Myles meant when he said something had happened in his life that he couldn't prevent. He told me he'd done his best to repair the damage, how on earth do you go about repairing something like that?'

'This might help to take your mind off it,' Pippa said, 'a furniture van's just pulled up. Your desk must have arrived.'

'Morning love, we've a desk for you from Romney's. Where do you want it?'

'Right here please. It's to replace this counter.'

The desk was duly installed and then the van driver asked her to sign for it. 'There's a bit of a mystery surrounding this desk,' he winked.

'Oh god, not another one,' Lydia snapped, and he stepped back a pace in surprise.

'It's no big deal,' he stammered, 'Mr. Romney wanted you to know he'd found the secret drawer when he was restoring it, that was all. These types of desks always have them, the trick's in finding them see. The boss wanted to make sure you knew where it was.' He gave her the top copy of the signed document, 'There you are love, we'll leave you to it,' and he made his way out of the shop. Moments later he came back carrying a small, strong box, in his hand, 'Almost forgot this, it was in the secret drawer. You'll need a locksmith mind, there's no key.'

Natalie was beginning to feel pleased with her investigations so far. If they'd been testing her ability as a detective, she'd delivered the goods. Now she needed to discover how Myles had ended up in America with a bride. She'd drawn a blank with marriages registered in Britain for Myles Barringham around that time. He wasn't listed on any British census either and she'd lost all trace of Polly Brown since she'd left the workhouse. It was proving difficult finding a descendent or anyone with personal information about the Barringham family, people travelled far and wide and between the time when Polly left the workhouse and now, there had been another world war, and after the war the assisted passage to Australia. Natalie decided to cast her net further, she put advertisements in the British national newspapers and those in Australia, New Zealand and Canada, asking for anyone with information about Polly Brown or Myles Barringham to contact her. She would have to be patient waiting for the responses to come in, but her mind wasn't idle. She mentally ran through the facts so far. Myles had found Polly and the baby, then the trail had ended. Was he her lover? Or was he in league with his father. Had he killed Polly and the baby to end all possibility of exposing Barringham as a murderer? No, that was too horrific to contemplate. Supposing then, that Myles had been the good guy, how had he known where to find Polly? And would she have trusted him enough to tell him what had happened to Frederick? Supposing she had. What could Myles have done about it? What could anyone have done, after learning that their father was a madman and a powerfully influential one at that? She thought for a moment... hide, that would have been her first instinct anyway, but how, and where?

'John what would you do, if you wanted to disappear, in the Nineteen-Twenties?'

'How do you mean disappear?'

'I mean make yourself disappear from society, with a woman and child in tow?'

'Change my name. Either just call myself something different or change it by deed pole. Either way it wouldn't leave much of a trail. Before computers, it would have been like looking for a needle in a haystack, unless the authorities happened to fall lucky on a piece of information. I don't know how much of a data base was kept nationally. There was national insurance but no health service. Technology was advancing in the twenties but they obviously didn't have anything like the resources we have today. I expect they relied on advertising and tip offs to track people down.

'What an oversight, I should have realised he'd changed his identity, I never asked what the great-grandfather was called.' She picked up her phone and sent a text to Grant. His reply was instant.

'Alright,' she said, after reading his answer, 'Stevenson is the mother's name. She added it to her married name and became Stevenson-Granger. Apparently, Grant Stevenson has dropped the Granger. So, we're looking for Myles Stevenson.

Grant said his Gramps was called Eric. Is that a derivative of Frederick? And what of Polly, do you think she simply liked the name Lydia?'

Natalie ran the new information through the genealogy website's marriage register. 'Spot on!' she shouted, punching the air. John looked up from reading his paper, gave it a shake and went back to it.

Excited now, Natalie checked the passenger logs of ships departing from the south of England for America, shortly after the date of the marriage. Nothing. She leaned back in her chair rubbing her neck and aching shoulders, 'Do you want a glass of wine?' she said, 'I've drawn a blank.'

'Have you tried ships leaving from Liverpool?' he said, 'Go on, I'll open the bottle, you get looking.'

'Cheers,' she said, taking the glass. 'You've just solved part of the mystery. Look there.'

'Lead passenger Myles Stevenson,' he read, 'Spouse Lydia Fay Stevenson and Infant son Eric Stevenson. We make a good team, maybe I should retire and we could join forces?'

'I'm not sure I'd recommend this job,' she laughed.

Natalie had intended waiting to see if she got any information from her advertisements before she told Lydia and Grant about finding Myles, Polly and baby Frederick on the passenger list of a ship bound for New York. However, a few days later she happened to be driving by Lydia's shop. John's golf club had organised a charity fundraiser. It was to be a masked ball and she wanted to wear something more glamorous than she could find in her wardrobe. On impulse, she parked the car and went inside.

'This is a social visit,' she said, and watched Lydia's face relax into a smile. 'I need a dress for a masked ball. Nothing too elaborate, that's not my style and I'll need to get some wear out of it. I don't usually buy special occasion clothes.' Lydia gave her a selection of basic shift dresses to try on for colour and size. Then she explained to Natalie how the detail could be added or removed depending on the glamour of the occasion. That way she would get the most wear from her dress. She settled on an electric blue. The colour picked out the blue of her eyes and looked stunning with her ebony hair.

'Wow, no wonder customers flock to buy from you. You're a magician!'

'Not quite. The secret is in listening to what the client wants and using my experience to match their requirements.'

The bell over the door jingled and Pippa called out, 'It's only me,' Lydia stuck her head out of the changing room. 'I'm doing a dress fitting for Natalie Jacobs. Did you collect the strong box from the locksmith?'

'I did, and I think you'd both better come and read the contents.'

'What's all this about?' Natalie asked, following Lydia, still wearing the blue dress.

'I bought this desk from the vicarage,' Lydia said, stroking its surface. The Reverend told me it had originally belonged to the village Doctor and it was donated to the vicarage when the practice moved to the medical centre. The furniture restorer found that box in a secret drawer in the desk. It's been at the locksmith's because it was locked and without a key.'

'Here, read this letter,' Pippa said, it was the only thing in the box.' Lydia took the envelope and handed it to Natalie. She unfolded the letter and placed it on the desk smoothing out the creases.

'To whom it may concern,' she read out.

'I Doctor Matthew Trent, being of sound mind and limb, this day the 24th of May, 1917, do hereby bare my soul and appease my conscience in the hope that one day the truth will out and justice shall prevail. Though I fear, coward that I am, it shall not be during my lifetime. Nevertheless, I do solemnly declare, that late yesterday evening, I was called upon by Lord Barringham of Barringham Hall, Meadow Bank, to attend to his son, Frederick, who had been wounded in the abdomen from the discharge at close range of a shotgun. Little could be done for the poor fellow; stemming the massive blood loss would have made little difference to the outcome, since his vital organs had been shattered beyond repair.

When I would have reported the incident to the police, as the usual course of procedure, Lord Barringham informed me that it was a family matter and that should I report the incident to the police or anyone outside the confines of that room, he, Lord Barringham would prosecute me for malpractice and professional misconduct, conducive to imprisonment.

Lord Barringham is a respected Magistrate and I am left in little doubt that this was no idle threat. As a deeply religious man I have spent many hours in prayer searching my conscience. At last, I have reached a decision which has prompted me to write this letter. First and foremost, I believe that Lord Barringham will be punished, in the sense that not a moment shall pass when he does not berate himself. Secondly, had Frederick gone off to fight as planned that day, I am certain, knowing for where he was bound, that he would have been most fortunate indeed to have survived. Lastly and the reason closest to my heart, is my own family, where responsibility for their welfare weighs heavily upon my shoulders. Not only am I responsible for the care of my beloved wife and our three children, but also for the welfare of my dear widowed sister and her five children, also victims of this wretched war.

My decision made, I shall carry on with my life and duty as best as my conscience will allow, in the hope that someday, somehow, justice will prevail.

Yours faithfully
Matthew Trent MD'

'Well that pretty much confirms our findings so far.' Natalie said. 'If the letter is genuine of course?'

'What are you suggesting? That Pippa wrote the note? It was me who asked the Reverend if I could buy the desk. No-one tried to sell it to me. The furniture restorer found the box and a locksmith opened it. Or are you suggesting the Reverend is in league with our scam now?'

'Point taken, but keep an open mind is all I'm saying.'

'If my mind was any more open my brain would fall out,' she glared at Natalie.

'Would you like some tea?' Pippa said, trying to diffuse the situation in the only way she knew. If you leave the dress in the changing room I can box it up for you while you drink your tea. I'll bring a tray through to the office, shall I? She nodded pointedly at Lydia, willing her to calm down.

'That would be lovely, thank you,' Natalie said, accepting the peace offering.

The three women were still sitting around the office desk drinking tea and sharing a packet of chocolate digestives when Grant telephoned.

'Hi,' he said. 'I've had a report back from the pathologist. Frederick's body was recognisable from his injuries; the blast had shattered his spine. There wasn't much left of the uniform but his buttons and identity number were intact. His DNA is a match. There was another soldier in the crypt as well. The authorities have discovered who he was from his identity number. He was a man called Cartwright, his address was given as Barringham Hall and he came to work there as a servant from the orphanage where he'd lived. He must have been Frederick's batman in the army. Maybe it was Cartwright's body inside the coffin brought back from France. If he was an orphan, no-one would be looking for him.'

'Natalie is here with me. I'll pass on that information. By the way, there was a letter in that strong box they found in the desk's secret drawer. It was from the doctor who attended Frederick. Lord Barringham threatened him with a malpractice suit if he told anyone that Frederick had died from a shot gun wound in England. You can read the letter for yourself next time I see you.'

'This is like a jigsaw when all the pieces suddenly fit into place. I've spoken with Reverend Byewaters about the funeral. We thought it would be respectful to hold a service for both Frederick and Cartwright. I'll e-mail the dates and information across to you and Natalie. I'll probably drive over to yours tonight if that's OK. I'd like to see that letter. Shall I bring in a curry?'

'Sounds good, say about eight?'

The day of Frederick's funeral was a befitting one. Fog had bleached colour from the landscape, draping itself across hedgerows and hovering above the grass. The corsage proceeded to the church along streets lined with bystanders, alerted by the press. Grant had tried to keep the ceremony low key, but as he'd expected, the press had got wind of it. A tale of gentry, a Magistrate at that, murdering his son and heir, a local war hero, made good press. Mixed with the romantic aspect of the tragedy, the tale had reached the nationals. There had been something of a police presence on the

225

lychgate when the corsage arrived, preventing the ghouls from pressing forward and into the church. The solid oak doors were firmly closed against the outside world as the compassionate service was conducted by Reverend Byewaters.

In the early evening, Lydia stood in the bay window of Grant's private suite watching the rain pour down. A sudden flash of lightening alerted her to imminent thunder. 'At least the rain has lifted the fog.'

` 'Oh hell, I've left the hood down,' he said, grabbing his car keys.

'Won't the remote work from here?' she called out, 'Presumably not,' she said, as he disappeared from the room. She turned back to look out of the window at a display of fork lightening, too far away to be intimidating. Grant returned soaked through, his shirt was transparent, revealing his toned body. Hearing her gasp, he looked up, puzzled, 'It's turned cooler out there,' he said, brushing wet hair away from his eyes.

'You must be frozen!' she said, babbling out the first thing that came into her head, 'I'll get you a towel.'

'Don't bother, honey, I'm going to take a hot shower.'

The image that conjured up, sent a shiver down her spine. What's wrong with me? she thought. How can I desire two men living a hundred years apart? Hysteria over came her, the tension of the day had tipped her over the edge. She was laughing and crying at the same time, convinced this was the start of the break down she'd always known would come. She was wrong, by the time Grant had finished showering she was back in control and feeling much better for having had a good cry. If he noticed her puffy eyes, he didn't mention it. He was fully dressed but his hair was still damp. 'I'd half expected you to be gone,' he smiled, making her feel guilty for her past lame excuses. 'Stay to dinner,' he said. 'We can eat here or in the dining room, your call.'

'Thank you, that would be lovely,' she replied, and meant it. 'Would you mind if I take a shower before dinner? I feel drained and a bit hot and bothered. The service was very emotional, wasn't it?'

'It was, let's hope his soul can rest in peace now and Myles Barringham leaves us in peace.' Instantly the lights dipped and flickered. Lydia's eyes widened in surprise.

'It's the storm,' Grant laughed.

'I'd better take that shower, before the electricity goes off.'

They dined on the hotel terrace. The evening was warm and sultry, heavy with the threat of thunder. Subtle lighting illuminated the trees and plants surrounding the outdoor dance floor and moonlight shimmered on its marble surface, creating a glittering wonderland.

'We've captured a little bit of magic here,' she sighed.

'Shall we try it out,' he said, taking her hand. A slow foxtrot was playing and as they reached the bottom of the steps Grant gathered her into his arms and expertly guided her across the floor. His aftershave was a subtle blend of citrus and musk, invigorating yet sensual. 'This is real, this is now. No dreams, no ghosts,' he whispered. He was holding her so close, the heat of his skin penetrated her dress, as they clung together in silhouette against the moonlight.

The music faded and the spell was broken. 'Come on,' he said, 'I've an idea. Let's see if you approve.' Back in his apartment Grant opened the French doors and stepped onto the balcony. He pointed to an alcove she hadn't noticed before, 'Wait there,' he said, and disappeared back inside. Suddenly the balcony was bathed in light, revealing that the large shape in the corner was a hot tub. The top opened by remote to expose the bubbling, steaming water. 'No skinny dipping required,' he winked, handing her a swimsuit. 'Unless you insist of course.'

'Thank you for considering my modesty,' she laughed, and reached up to kiss his cheek. In a flash, he'd captured her lips, her response was instant and her body moulded to his as he crushed her to him…

'Room service sir!' the voice was coming from the living room.

'Damn,' he cursed, breaking away from the kiss, his eyes glittered with desire, 'That'll be the Champagne, I must have left the door open.' He returned carrying a bottle on ice. 'Geez,' he said, when he saw that she'd changed into the swimsuit. 'I sure can't guarantee gentlemanly conduct while you're wearing that, honey.'

She stepped into the hot tub and he handed her a fluted glass of Champagne, then he stepped in beside her. 'Here's to the future,' he said, raising his glass and taking a sip, 'And to us,' he added, leaning over to kiss her.

The ice in the bucket had all but melted, when next they poured from the bottle.

Chapter Twenty-Five

Natalie Jacobs was up bright and early, refreshed after a good night's sleep. John had been working a night shift and as much as she loved him, it had been nice to spread out in the bed.

Donning a tracksuit, she set off for a jog around the park. The activity helped order her thoughts. Her first thought was of Beryl Marsh and her revelation about Lord Barrington shooting his son, Frederick. The second was that Beryl might possibly be in league with Grant Stevenson, even though they had both denied knowing one another. Then she wondered how, if the story was true, had Barringham and the gamekeeper managed to get the body back into the house unnoticed. Did Barringham have such a tyrannical grip on all his servants? She was busy pondering the facts when her mobile rang. It was Lydia Lockwood. 'Hi, sorry to phone so early, but you did say any time. I need to tell you something. I suppose I probably should have spoken to you sooner, but the first two occasions seemed irrelevant and the last one well… it's just that I've been so busy. No, that's just an excuse. I haven't contacted you before now, because I feel embarrassed.'

'Sorry Lydia, you've lost me. What is it that you're trying to tell me?'

'I've had several more hallucinations.'

Natalie could hear the anxiety in Lydia's voice, 'Alright,' she said, 'Let's start from the beginning. Take your time I'm in no hurry.'

Lydia began by telling Natalie about the voice she'd heard in the car, warning her about the argumentative architect, and then the mysterious horse rider saving her life.

Natalie listened patiently before offering her opinion. 'It's no surprise that the first architect proved to be unsuitable. On projects of that magnitude I image it happens quite often. Although I don't have an answer for who spoke to you in the car. Unless you were so engrossed in working through the plans that you mistook your thoughts for reality.' The explanation sounded weak even to her ears, and she gave more consideration to her next offering. 'The rider you saw is more easily explained. You were riding out after Grant and Jenny, right? So, do you think, that when a male rider came galloping to the rescue, you expected it to be Grant? The brain seems programmed to see what we expect to see. When the riding instructor told you it wasn't Grant, you automatically assumed it must have been Myles, because they look so similar. Surely when you saw the rider on the hill lifting his hat, he wasn't close enough for you to see his features?'

Lydia was forced to agree that the explanation was a good analysis. Taking a deep breath, she finally managed to divulge everything that had happened after meeting Myles at the garden party.

Natalie listened gravely to the details, reverting to her first impression that Lydia was a sadly deranged woman. She had run out of explanations for Lydia's fantasies. One fact, however, leaped from the fantasy to tie in with her investigations.

'This secret passage. Would it have been big enough for two men to carry a third up to the bedroom?'

'Quite easily, I should think, why?'

'Because I'm presuming that's the way the gamekeeper and Lord Barringham got Frederick back into the house. They must have smuggled the doctor in and out that way as well and it's probably how they managed to get the body undetected into the crypt. Lydia, are you being straight with me? You and Grant Stevenson keep coincidentally coming up with facts that can be confirmed. It's making me suspicious. Are you testing me? I'm yet to be convinced that I'm not at the centre of a practical joke. Please be careful if it's a game you're playing. As I've already told Grant, I'm a better detective than you're both giving me credit for. I will find out the truth.'

'Yes, that's what Myles said.'

'Who? Oh, you mean the ghost.'

'Natalie, I know you're finding it difficult to believe in us. I can understand that, especially when I don't even know myself what's real and

232

what isn't. All I do know, is that the information I've given to you is something that I've experienced. Whether it's fact or merely a hallucination, that's what we've hired you to find out.'

That's told me, Natalie thought, putting the phone back in her jacket pocket and zipping it up. She stood for a few moments breathing the fresh morning air. The park was deserted, just how she liked it. Presumably when Frederick hadn't reported for duty, he would have been registered as AWL. How could Barringham have got around that? She set off jogging again. She was on her second lap around the lake when she was stopped dead in her tracks by the memory of the fire in the records office. Of course, he must have had help on the inside. How convenient, but what hold did Barringham have over his accomplice? She looked at her watch. John should be home from his nightshift. There would be time for breakfast together before he went off to bed.

She walked into the kitchen to the smell of toast and bacon.

'I read your note,' John said, 'Do you want some scrambled eggs with this bacon? There's a coffee over there, I've not drunk from it yet.'

She took the plate from him and sat at the breakfast bar next to the mug of coffee.

'Did you have a good shift?'

'Not bad, quiet really. Still, it gave me a chance to catch up on some paper work,' he said, pulling a face as he spooned the scrambled eggs onto her plate. He poured himself a coffee and joined her. 'How was your evening?'

'Not as productive as this morning,' and she told him about Lydia's phone call and her thoughts on the cover up of Frederick's murder. John listened as he tucked into his breakfast. 'It might be a good idea to read through the newspaper archives again before you go dashing off to the National Archive Office. Go through any coverage on the body being brought back from France and the memorial service with a fine-tooth comb. You might pick up on a snippet of information or a name you missed the first time around.'

'Message received and understood, Guv,' she said, standing up and kissing the top of his head before she snatched the last triangle of toast from his plate.

'Have a good rest,' she said, clearing the breakfast bar and stacking the dish washer, 'I doubt I'll be back from London before you're back on the night shift, but I'll let you know I'm home in one piece.'

'So, you're going anyway,' he said.

'Got to I'm afraid, gut feeling won't let me rest.'

By the time the train had pulled into St. Pancras station, Natalie had set out an investigation plan and typed up a report of her findings so far. Closing the laptop and gathering her things, she made her way to the carriage door, ready to leap from the train the moment it stopped. The onward trains were frequent and she arrived at her destination quite easily. As she'd predicted, Barringham had previously been in the same regiment as his son. She read through his records. He'd fought in the Boer War as a Captain and he'd been commended for bravery, for saving the life of a young officer at risk to his own. Perhaps he hadn't always been an evil so-and-so, she thought. Making a note of the officer's name, she then looked up his records. His career had taken him to the height of Major by the time he retired from the army at the end of the First World War. Now we're getting somewhere, she pressed a finger to her lips in concentration. Just how grateful would a Major be to a retired Captain for saving his life? Surely, he wouldn't be grateful enough to risk his career and reputation, not to mention a probable prison sentence. No, there had to be more to it than that. What other hold could Barringham have over him?

She checked the records again; more carefully this time. Nothing noteworthy appeared at first but then a pattern began to emerge. Every few months a complaint would be logged, a complaint of a homosexual nature against the young officer. In each case the complaint had been quashed by Barringham providing a valid excuse for the officer's behaviour. Only carrying out orders, checking on homosexual activities amongst the ranks. Various excuses amounting to the same thing. Had Barringham been covering for the young officer? Or had he been setting him up by inventing evidence to hold against him later? Natalie could well imagine that a man vile enough to murder his own son would relish having his own creature. She wondered how many others there'd been. She handed the ledger back and arranged for copies of the relevant pages to file with her report. She felt disgusted. By the time Frederick was serving in that Regiment the young officer would have become his Major and Barringham had him over a barrel. The poor man would have been damned if he did, and damned if he didn't. If he'd helped Barringham disguise his son's murder, and been caught, he'd have been charged. If he'd refused, Barringham would have exposed him as a homosexual; a charge which carried a prison sentence in those days. It would seem then, that the Major had taken the risk of not being caught as an accomplice, and helped Barringham cover up the murder.

She looked at her watch. If she could get through the rush hour crowds to catch the next train, she'd be home before John left for work, but she wanted to see if Myles had a war record first. It took a while to find him. Eventually she discovered that he had been Air Corp. He'd flown spy planes as part of intelligence, but interestingly quite a few sections of his records were missing, replaced with blank pages stamped classified. She read that he was fluent in German and French. Had he been operating behind enemy lines? Was that why the missing information was marked classified or had they simply not bothered updating his file, if not, why not? That war was a century ago. What was available read like the stuff from a Biggles adventure, hardly credible. Myles Barringham it seemed had been a hero. And no-one knew. He was simply known as a notorious playboy and the black sheep of the family.

She arrived at St. Pancras station with only minutes to spare. She managed to squeeze onto the platform just as the barriers were closing and climbed onto the crowded train feeling grateful she'd reserved a seat.

Her phone rang as the train was pulling away from the station. It was John. 'Just wondered how you were getting on?' he said.

'I'm on the early train, I should be back before you leave.'

'That's good, how about I meet you off the train and we grab something to eat at the Italian?'

'Sounds perfect. Hold on a minute love,' she said, making her way to the toilet. 'Sorry about that, I couldn't talk in there, the carriage is full.'

'Regular sleuth, you are,' he laughed, when she told him where she was speaking from.

'I've found a connection between a Major serving at the time of Frederick's death and Barringham. The Major would have had access to burn the records and cover Barringham's trail. I'll tell you about it over dinner. It's not very pleasant in here.'

Pleasant or not, now she was in there she felt the urge to use the facilities. She washed her hands and quickly refreshed her make-up, adding a spray of perfume before returning to her seat. She typed her new findings in the report she'd written on the outward journey and then sent an email to both Lydia and Grant.

Chapter Twenty-Six

Standing on Grant's private balcony, Lydia put on a hotel robe, and wrapped it tightly around her. A gold and scarlet sunrise was spreading over the horizon. Behind her Grant was sleeping peacefully. His sun-bleached hair glistening in the half light.

You're beautiful, she thought, kind, funny, intelligent. Perfect really, except… you're not him. She looked to the horizon again, hot tears spilling down her cheeks. 'Where are you, Myles?' she cried out, and her voice bounced off the drab walls of the housing estate and echoed away into the distance. Spinning around she dropped to the floor hugging her knees and sobbed as though her heart would break.

Warm hands cupped her elbows lifting her to her feet and strong arms enfolded her until her head was resting against a muscular chest. She looked up, expecting to see Grant, but it was Myles whose eyes were gazing so lovingly into hers. He stroked the damp tendrils away from her face and brushed the tears from her cheeks. He kissed her softly and her world tilted; everything felt right.

'Come with me,' he said. Taking her hand, he walked around the bed where Grant was sleeping. 'Don't worry about him. An hour or the merest blink of an eye, it's all subjective between parallels,' and then he opened the wardrobe door.

'Where are you taking me now? she said, 'Narnia?' The joke was lost on him.

'No, breakfast. There are a couple of people I'd like you to meet. But first you need to get dressed, take your pick. I'll be waiting for you on the landing.'

After further inspection, Lydia discovered that the wardrobe contained a collection of vintage clothes, not dissimilar to her own designs. Intrigued by this turn of events, she quickly showered and changed into a hyacinth blue costume with white collar and cuffs. She selected a hat to match the costume and as it was summer, white gloves. Then, folding a lightweight Mackintosh over her arm, she walked onto the landing to meet Myles.

'You look marvellous, darling,' he said, jumping up from the chaise longue, 'Absolutely top notch.' Taking her hand, he proudly tucked it under his arm and together they descended the now familiar magnificent staircase.

Myles ushered her into the breakfast room and Lydia's eyes were immediately drawn to the collection of huge silver platters covered by dome lids and set out across the longest sideboard she had ever seen.

'There's porridge and bacon, with a choice of eggs,' he said, fussing around her like a school boy bringing a favoured friend home for the first time. Do you like them fried, scrambled or poached, with sausages or kippers?' he asked, lifting the lid of each platter in turn to reveal the contents as he worked his way along the line.

Engrossed, Lydia didn't at first notice the room's other occupants.

'For heaven's sake, Myles, give the poor girl a chance to make her choice. I'm feeling quite breathless just listening to you.'

Lydia turned to see who had spoken. Sitting at the table, his back ramrod straight was a young man almost the image of Myles. Beside him sat the beautiful Lady Barringham.

'Good morning, my dear,' the man said, rising to his feet, 'Lord Frederick Barringham – Freddie,' he smiled, holding out his hand. Lydia clasped it and tears stuck in her throat as she looked on the handsome face of the man who'd been murdered in his prime and whose remains, she had only recently seen blessed and committed to a crypt. He seemed embarrassed, as though reading her thoughts. Retrieving his hand, he said, 'And this is my lovely wife, whom I believe you've already met.'

Lydia turned to Myles and mouthed '*his* wife?' he simply winked at her and grinned. She realised Lady Barringham was speaking to her and turned to apologise, 'I'm sorry, I didn't quite catch what you were saying?'

'I was asking you, to call me Polly. Please do, won't you? Everyone does around here you know.' And she jumped up from the breakfast table and handed Lydia a plate. 'Come on, I'll take you through it again, at a more leisurely pace,' she said, giving Myles a stern look.

With Polly's help, Lydia piled up her plate and managed to put it down on the table only moments before her legs buckled. The timely butler slid a chair under her bottom and she landed with a thump.

'A strong sweet tea, for Miss Lockwood, please Cartwright,' Myles instructed the footman who had entered the room carrying a fresh pot of tea and hot water. 'She's had a bit of a shock.' Cartwright poured the tea and the butler placed it beside her breakfast plate.

'Cartwright was in Freddie's regiment during the war,' Myles said, 'Got pretty bashed up by all accounts. But now, thanks to you, and Grant and Natalie of course, he's back here and married to his sweetheart.'

Lydia recognised the name. He was the other soldier discovered in the crypt. She turned to look at Freddie who was standing with his arm around Polly's waist. 'And Frederick, I mean Freddie, is with his sweetheart.' she said, 'You were the couple in Grant's dream, weren't you?'

'That's right my dear.'

'So, where am I? Is this place heaven?'

'You're seeing a parallel dimension, the place where we've chosen to exist.'

'But surely,' she said, turning to Cartwright, 'it can't be your idea of bliss, continuing to live as a servant?'

'Well now, Miss, I'm not rightly a servant no more. I'm just continuing doing the job I've always enjoyed. Me and my Connie, she's the lady's maid now that Polly is Lady Barringham. We like it here, we've a nice cottage on the estate and hoping for some nippers to join us afore long. You're right though, Miss. This wouldn't be everyone's cup of tea, I'll admit that, but you see we can do as we please if no harms done. And it pleases me and Connie to be here.' He turned to the butler, 'Will that be all for now, Mr. Williams?' Then with a slight bow he left the room.

The hot tea and breakfast fortified Lydia enough to ask more questions, 'I'm curious to know,' she said, 'if your name's Polly, and you are Fredericks sweetheart, why you were known as Lady Lydia Fay Barringham in the portrait and married to Myles?' She was disappointed with the answer.

'Life has its complications,' Polly beamed. 'All will be revealed soon enough and the pieces of the puzzle will come together.'

'I think you'll find,' Frederick confirmed, 'that Natalie Jacobs has gathered more information for you. She'll be in touch within a day or so.'

'If you've finished,' Myles said, 'I'd like to take you on a tour of the house.' The butler immediately stepped forward to pull out her chair.

She followed Myles from room to room in a daze. Everywhere was a replica of the hotel since its transformation to the art Decco style, yet here it was a private residence and looked as she remembered it that first time she had run down the staircase on Midsummer's Eve. She laughed remembering her assumption that the view from the landing window had been a holographic projection although the truth was far less believable. The most difficult job in refurbishing the hotel had been locating the rare pieces of furniture. In the end, Grant had settled for replicas. She marvelled that here in this existence, she was seeing the originals.

'I'm still very confused,' she said, 'You told me that Lady Barringham – Polly – had visited my shop many times before the day I actually saw her. Did she not come through to this dimension at the same time as you?'

'She didn't move on like me. Frederick was earth bound, and although she couldn't reach him, she wanted to stay as close by as possible. You and Grant helped me bring them together again.'

'I thought that by refurbishing the hotel from minimalist to Art Deco, we were refurbishing the building because it would appear that way to you in your existence, but this was already here, this is just how I first saw it on Midsummer's Eve, so what was the point of refurbishing the hotel, twice?'

'I feel I was ultimately responsible for my family's ruin and the building's downfall. This outcome has preserved the building for the foreseeable future. But my main reason for the restoration was to make the building the nucleus in bringing everyone together to uncover the murder. The building was hiding the secret of Frederick's death as well as his body.'

'So, have you fulfilled your mission? I mean, you left your dimension to expose your father as a murderer and reveal how Frederick died, right? We thought it would help him and Cartwright to have a proper burial service, and from what I've seen, it seems to have worked. He and Polly, and Cartwright and his Connie are together, and this dimension is pretty much set up how I presume you intended it to be.'

'Perfect for everyone, everyone except me. Lydia, I know you can remember what you wished for, but can you remember why you made that wish?'

'Because I, well, I suppose it was, I don't know,' she lied. Taken by surprise, she couldn't form the words that she wanted to say. 'Can we go outside? I need some air.'

The grounds were unexpectedly superb. Far larger than the present day, and set against the backdrop of gentle rolling hills. Not the drab housing estate she was used to seeing. In the centre of the gardens was an ornamental lake with a giant water fountain cascading over bronze mermaids riding dolphins. Myles and Lydia stood a while watching rainbows in the spray. She thought how often she had wished to live the simple, genteel existence of a bygone age, and wondered why she felt so at odds with the rest of modern society. Or why she felt so utterly comfortable in the vintage world with which she surrounded herself. She thought of Myles' question and the wish she'd made on the shooting star. It seemed so long ago, and yet no time at all, since she'd wished to live in the kind of world Myles had presented her with. He was a handsome chivalrous English gentleman who cherished her. He was precisely what she'd wished for.

She looked up into his anxious face and saw the hint of a hopeful smile tugging at his mouth. 'I wished for you, and everything you are,' she said, 'That'll teach me to be careful what I wish for, my gallant English gentleman.'

'Your wish was my passport here my darling, and it is also your passport to making your dreams come true. I can't guide you, you have to find your own way.' He stood staring at her, he seemed to be willing her to remember something. Eventually he sighed and turned away. 'Come on,

I'll walk you back.' They walked hand in hand through the gardens as far as the perimeter of the building. Then they stepped onto the dance floor and into the present time. Together they walked on, and up the stone steps. The day promised to be warm and fine and the hotel staff had begun laying the breakfast buffet on the terrace. She hadn't realised until now how thirsty she was and she poured orange juice into two of the glasses.

Myles came to stand behind her and kissed the nape of her neck, sending chills along her spine. 'Find your way home, Lydia,' he whispered, wrapping his arms around her waist, 'I miss you.'

She turned within the circle of his arms and saw that he was looking at her in that strange way he had of seemingly searching her soul.

'You have until midnight on Midsummer's Eve to find me,' he said. 'After that, our existence will run parallel, but never again coincide. This is our one and only chance.' He took both glasses from her and set them down on the table, then he wrapped his arms around her, and kissed her with such intensity that he bruised her lips. Abruptly he set her apart and strode purposefully towards the steps. At the top, he turned and saluted before dropping down them two at a time. She rushed after him, and watched him vanish as his feet touched the last step.

She trailed back through the hotel and up the stairs. How symbolic this staircase had

247

become since the first time she'd run down it. In a few weeks' time, it would be central to Pippa and Nick's wedding. With a start, she wondered whether this was the portal to the earths parallel dimension. Myles had said to find her way home. Was home the place where she would find Frederick and Polly, and Cartwright, and more importantly Myles? She stood still, willing the staircase to swallow her up and whisk her away.

She found Grant still asleep, exactly as Myles had promised. The time on the clock said 6..55AM. It was a shock to realise only moments had passed in this dimension. She jumped as the telephone rang. Grant reached out to answered it, still half asleep. She watched, fascinated by his ability to become instantly alert as he registered what the caller was saying. 'What? The New York hotel's what? OK, OK, calm down. I'll catch the next flight out.'

Not wishing to eavesdrop, she went through to the living room and ordered him coffee and bacon rolls to go. When she returned to the bedroom he was already showered and dressed.

'Sorry honey,' he shrugged. 'It looks like I'm gonna be across the pond for a few days,'

'I ordered you breakfast to go from room service. I'll drive you to the airport if you like?'

'Thanks for the offer, but I have a courtesy car on standby.' He took her into his arms and kissed her. 'I'll try not to be away too long. OK kiddo, I gotta go.' He picked up his flight bag and opened the door, almost colliding with the porter's fist, poised to knock. Hitching the flight bag over his shoulder, Grant grabbed the bacon roll and carton of coffee and jogged along the corridor. She signed the receipt for room service, and picked up her own coffee and roll. Taking a sip, she turned into the room and kicked the door shut with her heel. She was still wearing the hyacinth blue costume and hat. Grant hadn't even noticed. 'Cheers Myles,' she said, lifting her coffee cup in salute to her reflection.

Chapter Twenty-Seven

Lydia was too busy with last minute wedding preparations to worry about Grant, or even Myles for that matter. Then at the height of it all, Natalie Jacobs phoned to say she'd completed her investigations, and would like to discuss her findings and hand over her report. A few days before the wedding, she came into the shop. Lydia took her through to the office, Pippa went to organise tea and coffee, and while she was making it, she asked a couple of the workroom girls to cover the shop so she could go into the meeting.

Natalie took a sip of her coffee and put it down on the desk, 'Myles Barringham,' she began, 'changed his surname by deed poll to Stevenson and married Polly Brown.'

'So, who was Lydia Fay?'

'She was Myles fiancé. She was killed during the First World War while serving as a nurse in France. Polly needed a new identity, perhaps they chose that name in honour of her memory.'

'Does that mean that Myles was the father of Polly's baby after all?'

'I had assumed so, until a descendent of Polly's read my appeal for information in the newspaper and contacted me. They confirmed that Frederick was the father. It seems that Myles had visited Polly's family in secret, before leaving for America. He explained that Polly had been the love of Frederick's life and that his offer of marriage had been sincere. Myles told them then about his own fiancé, being killed in France, and admitted that he had asked Polly to marry him, to honour his brother's promise and give his child a legitimate name. He assured them that although he and Polly were not in love, they were very fond of each other, and he intended do his best to make her happy.

Not the most romantic of proposals, I'll admit, but very honourable and Polly wouldn't have had much option, in those days, other than to accept his offer, poor girl.'

'Did your contact say whether Myles had known about Polly and Frederick's plan to elope? Although I suppose even if he had known, he probably thought that Frederick would have provided for her, in case he was killed in France.'

'No, Myles hadn't known anything about it. He was out of the country at the time. I've discovered that Myles Barringham was something of a Scarlet Pimpernel during the First World War. He flew a spy plane and seems to have worked more closely with intelligence than was widely known. He was fluent in both German and French. The carefree playboy reputation was a cover, I think.

He found Polly quite by chance just at the end of the war. She'd been sent by the workhouse to collect a donation of clothes from a house in Kensington. He had been visiting friends next door. He told Polly's family, that when she saw him, she'd been so terrified she'd dropped her bundle in her haste to get away. He'd followed her to the workhouse and gone straight in to makes enquiries. He got her discharged under the guise of needing a housekeeper. Then he'd taken her straight to the nearest restaurant because he said she looked like she needed feeding up. Eventually, he coaxed her into telling him why she'd been so afraid. That's how he received the news that Frederick was dead and learned the gruesome truth behind his death.

After the meal, they went to the orphanage where baby Frederick had been sent to escape an outbreak of Diphtheria in the workhouse. Then they went in search of suitable accommodation to tide them over until they'd worked out what to do for the best. Polly stayed there with the baby, while Myles returned to Barringham Hall. His family had been expecting him and it also suited his plan. That's when he'd secretly met with Polly's family. He told them about the arrangements he'd made to begin a new life in America with a new identity and that he intended to take the deeds and jewels with him. He said that taking them, was the best way he could think of, to hit back at his father.'

'Everything's in the report,' Natalie said, tapping the file on the desk. 'The invoice for my services is in there as well. Anything you want explaining, just give me a call. This has been one of the most unusual cases I've handled and I'll admit I was reluctant to take it on at first, but I've enjoyed working on it in the end. I'm glad I've proved your ghosts existed as people, once, and that I've uncovered their story, even if I couldn't find proof of the ghosts themselves. Now that really would have been something.'

Getting to her feet, she said, 'There's no substantial evidence to say that an outsider is causing mischief with either company, but if you have further suspicions, and you'd like my help, you know where to find me.' They shook hands and Natalie left.

Outside, on the pavement, she paused. A movement in the shop window had caught her eye. A woman was waving at her from the chair in the window, she stepped forward to take a closer look, the chair was empty. She took a deep breath, I've been a hard nose cop for too long to believe in all that mumbo jumbo, she thought, striding off down the street, but she couldn't resist another peek as she turned the corner.

Grant returned in the early hours the day before the wedding. Lydia, Pippa and Jenny, had been at the hotel on and off for most of the previous week, organising the wedding preparations. The marquee was festooned with garlands of fresh flowers and foliage entwined with hundreds of tiny white lights. The bridal table was coordinated in the same way, with the addition of an elaborate centrepiece, a floral arrangement, studded with star lights, which covered the entire length of the table. Miniature replicas were placed at the centre of each of the guest's tables, surrounded by Edwardian style place cards, which opened into small fans to reveal the menu. The scent of roses and gardenia filled the marquee, eliminating any lingering smell of damp grass. An image of earth's galaxy was to be projected onto the roof of the marquee as a surprise reminder to the bride that her wish on a shooting star had come true.

Jenny and Lydia had arranged for Pippa to spend the day before her wedding in the hotel spa. She had strict instructions to use the service stairs and not come anywhere near the main staircase until the morning of the wedding. The decorating of the bridal walkway and arch were to be a surprise.

'It's a good job I trust the pair of you,' she grumbled as she packed her bag for the day.

'You know you'd only work yourself up into a nervous frenzy if you stayed,' Lydia told her. 'Go and relax, you deserve a day of pampering. You're the bride.'

That evening Lydia joined Grant on his private terrace for dinner. 'What would you like to drink?' he asked.

'White wine and soda, please, loaded with ice.'

As he gave her the glass, Billy jumped up to snap at a cloud of midges and almost knocked it out of her hand.

'Lie down Billy,' she ordered the dog, shaking droplets of wine from her fingers. 'I don't know what's wrong with him. He's had a good two hours in the woods and been running around here getting under everyone's feet all day.'

'He's reached that age,' Grant nodded knowingly. 'It's summer, he's full of wanderlust. I suggest you have a word with Nick when he's back from honeymoon.'

'Of course, I hadn't thought about that.'

She sat back in her chair sipping the cold drink, satisfied that after months of preparation, everything was in place for Pippa's wedding. She had worked her magic for her best friend.

'Did you get chance to read through Natalie Jacobs report?'

'I sure did, that was a turn up for the books, I wonder what my folks will make of it when I tell them my great-grandfather Myles turns out to be my great, great-uncle. Guess that makes me the true heir to Barringham Hall. Geez and it cost me a packet to buy it back,' he laughed.

'I wonder why Myles had the portraits painted and used the Barringham title on the plaques. after he'd gone to all that trouble to disguise his identity?'

'Can't really say, maybe he figured that after his parents died, it would be safe for him to come back and claim his inheritance. Presumably the building had been sold at some point with or without the deeds. Maybe he tried to buy it back and the new owner wouldn't sell. We may never know, but I can sure see why he changed his name in the first place and told a different story to the real one. I'm proud to call him a relative, he was one hell of a guy.'

'Yes, he was,' Lydia whispered.

Grant took a sip of wine and settled back in his chair, 'In Natalie's report,' he said, 'the immigration records show that Myles and his new family docked in New York. I wonder how long they stayed there, and what motivated them to move south?'

'New York's a big place, but an obvious choice. Perhaps he was still trying to cover his trail. He'd visited America before you know, he had his car shipped over from there. He could have been afraid of being recognised. He was probably well known in aristocratic circles.'

'You're frowning, what's up?'

'I've just realised something. That car he took me for a ride in was built in the mid -twenties and everything I saw at the Midsummers Eve Ball was early Art Deco. Myles would have been living in America by then. That means, I wasn't seeing into the past, I was seeing the present.'

'The present? In the twenties?'

'Not our present, a parallel present. If I've understood the concept. It's a place where souls

256

can choose to spend eternity in the existence of their choice. That outcome is affected by one's life on earth. Myles said that the people he most wanted to be with couldn't move on with him because of something that had happened in his lifetime. You know why he came through to our dimension. He needed to expose Frederick's death as a murder. Polly and Frederick were star crossed lovers, you see. They would have been married if his father hadn't shot him. The pieces of the jigsaw are coming together, just as Polly and Frederick predicted. Myles needed our help to bring his plan together. I suppose you could say we were his transmitters. It's great to know that even by Midsummer's Eve, last year, Myles parallel existence was beginning to take shape. But it took the discovery of the murder to bring Frederick and Polly together. Phew, I need another drink after that.'

Swallows dipped and dived foraging for insects and Billy jumped up again to chase them. The heady scent of roses wafted on the breeze; the essence of a summer's evening in England.

'Do you think we'll ever hear from Myles again now that we've exposed Frederick's murder?'

Lydia twirled the stem of her glass, 'I've really no idea,' she said, yet knowing for certain she would be seeing him quite soon. The scent of honeysuckle was thick in the air, like a fragrant signature tune. Draining her glass, she stood up, 'I'm going to bed, we've a big day tomorrow.'

'Goodnight, honey, I'll not be long for bed myself, I need to catch up on some sleep. The last few days have been hectic.'

She did not question why he hadn't suggested they share a room. She had only felt relief. After hanging up her clothes she slipped into a bathrobe and went to switch on the shower. Steam clouded the small room. Now that the wedding preparations were complete, she began to relax for the first time in weeks, her nerves felt completely frazzled. She stood with her hands on the rim of the wash basin breathing in the steamy atmosphere, it had a calming effect.

A flicker of movement caught her eye. She looked up to see the words, I love you, being scrawled in the steam on the mirror. Shocked, she staggered backwards and tumbled into the bath. Water from the shower cascaded down soaking her hair and bathrobe.

Instantly Myles appeared, 'My dear girl, are you hurt?' he said, offering his hand to haul her out. She took it, yanked hard and pulled him in.

'You did that on purpose,' he blustered.

'Yes, and you did that?' she said, pointing an accusing finger at the mirror.

'I thought it was rather a romantic gesture, don't you like it?'

'No, you scared me half to death, you numb skull.'

'Numb skull, am I? We'll see about that,' he said, pulling her close and kissing her thoroughly.

'Yes, well, don't do it again,' she said as he released her.

'Do you mean don't do this again?' he said, nibbling her ear, 'or this?' he nuzzled her neck, 'or this,' and he kissed her again.

She shoved hard against his chest. 'Will you get out of here? Incorrigible man!'

'Oh, so I'm incorrigible now.'

'I'm trying to get ready for bed.'

'I can help you with that,' he said, pulling her to standing and releasing the robe. He nudged it from her shoulder caressing her wet skin with his lips. The robe fell to her ankles, he followed its path with kisses and she cried out.

'Have you remembered your way home yet?' his voice sounded husky against her ear.

'I've no idea what you're talking about,' she gasped, as he nuzzled her neck, 'and even if I did, how could we possibly have a future together? It's been like speed dating a phantom!'

'I don't know what speed dating is, but if only you would try to remember, we could spend all eternity together. Come on Lydia, concentrate. Do you really not remember anything of before?'

The moment his words were out, he began to fade. 'Oh, my god, what have I done? My darling I'm so sorry, I've ruined it. After everything we've been through I've gone and blasted ruined it. I love you Lydia, always remember that. I love you now, and I have loved you for all eternity. Forgive me.'

'Where are you going? Don't leave me,' she pleaded. Her voice echoed in the empty room.

Chapter Twenty-Eight

Frantic knocking woke her from a deep sleep. For a moment, she had a sense of déjà vu, but Billy's loud barking brought her back to reality. She padded across to the door and opened it a crack.

'Wake up sleepy head, it's almost noon and the big day has arrived!' Pippa pushed passed her and went straight to the hospitality tray. 'God, you look awful,' she said, switching on the kettle, 'are you feeling alright?'

'I didn't have a good night. I think I was over tired when I went to bed,' she lied. She didn't see the point in upsetting Pippa by telling her that she'd cried until she'd fallen asleep, just as dawn was breaking. She crossed the room and opened the patio door to let Billy outside.

'Is it safe to let him out on his own?'

'Yes of course, it's a dog enclosure. It's fenced off and he's the only doggy guest this weekend.'

'Here,' Pippa said, handing her a cup of strong coffee, 'drink this, it will make you feel better. You should see it downstairs. The decorations are exquisite. There are garlands of white gardenia looped all the way up the staircase.'

'Yes, I do know,' Lydia laughed. 'Don't they smell heavenly?'

'They're covering the mantelpiece and the hearth, and they're sprouting everywhere from the candle sconces lining the aisle. How many are there?'

'I lost count, Grant had them flown in especially. There's one more surprise but you're not seeing that until you come down those stairs on your dad's arm.'

'You're so clever, Lydia. The Edwardian style I was hoping for has really come through.'

'I took inspiration from the Art Nouveau style of your dress. Your hair looks sensational by the way.'

'Thank you. I've come straight from the hairdressers.'

'Did you have it permed?'

'No, this is the real me. I've been straightening it for years.'

'Well, you had me fooled, and how long have I known you? Anyway, it's the perfect style for your dress, and curls are back in fashion. When do you want me to pin the flowers in your hair? Shall I do it now, or is it too early?'

'No, it's not too early, do it now please. I'd rather be prepared. There's no way they're going to fall out of this bird's nest.'

'Don't say that, it looks beautiful,' Lydia said, threading the flowers through the mass of curls tumbling down Pippa's back. She titivated the wispy tendrils framing her face and sprayed on some hair gloss to give it an extra sheen. Then she gave her the box containing the shooting star brooch, 'Your something borrowed,' she said.

Pippa wafted out of the room in a fragrant cloud of flowers and hairspray. Lydia locked the door behind her and then filled bowls of food and water for Billy and took them outside. He was nowhere to be seen. Probably in the bushes following a scent, she thought. She whistled, put the bowls down and went back indoors. In the bathroom, she switched on the shower and after taking stock of her face in the mirror, splashed cold water over her eyes to reduce the puffiness. The shower was hot and loosened off some of the tension in her shoulders. This is Pippa's day, she told herself. Time to dispatch Myles from my thoughts and focus on the day ahead.

Clever make-up disguised the red blotches on her face, and lashings of kohl and mascara minimised the look of puffiness around her eyes. Her hair had behaved itself for a change and dried in smooth waves. She shimmied into her dress to avoid getting make-up on it. The oyster silk tulle, with its smattering of spangles, complemented the bride's dress beautifully, but the tight fit was making it difficult to fasten the strap on her new shoes and she regretted not putting the shoes on first, but she hadn't wanted to risk tearing the hem with a heel.

She struggled even more with the gloves. She was all fingers and thumbs unfastening the tiny pearl buttons and then, because she was hot and sticky, the gloves wouldn't slide up her arms.

She wrenched them off in her temper and threw them across the bed, throwing herself down after them. She rolled over onto her back and pressed the heel of her hands into her forehead, willing the tears not to fall. She didn't have time to repair her make-up.

She ditched the gloves and went outside to cool off. There was still no sign of Billy. She looked down at his bowls, his food hadn't been touched. She looked around the enclosure calling and whistling, still no response. How could he have got out? She tiptoed around the perimeter, mindful of her Cuban heels sinking into the grass. Fear knotted her stomach as she spotted his escape route. He must have tunnelled his way under the wire fence. She ran back inside and phoned Grant.

'No, he's not with me, and I didn't see him in the grounds. I just got back from there, I've been checking that the caterers and waiting staff have everything ready.'

She ran down the staircase. The bridal arch, where Pippa and Nick would take their vows had been put in place, bringing a fresh new fragrance to the room. She checked with reception, but no one had seen Billy. She asked them to put the word out and then ran down the steps and into the car park. No sign. She ran around the perimeter of the building to where the marquee stood, asking everyone she passed if they'd seen her dog. If he'd come this far, there was a danger he could have run onto the road. Her heart thudded at the thought of him running onto the duel carriageway. Her shoes weren't designed for running, and the heels squeaked in protest. She pulled them off and ran barefoot to the edge of the road. A crowd had gathered on the opposite side of the carriageway, and her worst fears were realised when through a gap in the crowd she caught a glimpse of Billy's little brown and white body, lying lifeless at the kerb. She heard screaming. On and on it went. Then she was running, still unaware that she was the one screaming.

She ran straight into the road. Her only thought was that she had to get to Billy. The van that hit her knocked her clear over its roof and she bounced off the bonnet of the car behind. Tumbling with arms and legs flaying, she tried desperately to grasp hold of something solid; there was nothing but space. She was being sucked into a spiral of spinning golden light and the pain in her head was tremendous. Images of her life began whizzing through her mind. She saw her parents smiling proudly at her on graduation day and remembered the unbearable heat beneath her cap and gown. Then she was riding to the sixth form disco in the stretch limo, which her best friend's parents had hired, feeling sick and dizzy from her first taste of Champagne. As the chauffeur opened the car door, her date had stepped forward to take her hand. He'd later taken her heart and broken it. She saw herself dancing with him squashed together in the heaving mass of gyrating teenagers under a kaleidoscope of pulsating colour in time to the deafening rhythms.

Next, she saw her four-year-old self walking to school on her first day, how she had loathed the brown colour of that uniform and her new shoes had rubbed a blister. The following day she'd gone down with chicken pox. She saw herself paddling in the sea squealing as the cold waves rolled in over her legs, then earlier still, eating picnics in the park... Image after image raced backwards, further and further until finally her mind was blank. The spinning slowed and came to a standstill. Soothing golden light flowed into her body easing the pain in her head. The ground felt solid beneath her but other than that she felt nothing. She could hear voices and tried to make sense of what they were saying.

'She ran right out infront of me,' a man said, 'I hit the brakes, but I never stood a chance.'

'It's alright mate, you've enough witnesses here, we saw everything.'

She waited for the wave of pain to hit, it didn't come. She opened her eyes and looked up into the anxious faces gathered around. Billy was barking excitedly encouraging her to stand up. He was alive. She tentatively moved her arms, no pain. Then her legs. She tried to sit up.

'Has anyone phoned for an ambulance?' a man asked. His was the first voice she'd heard, presumably he was the driver.

'It's on its way mate, don't worry,' another man said, giving the driver a reassuring pat on the back.

Lydia struggled on to her elbow, 'No, please don't bother, I'm alright, really I am. If someone could just help me up?' No-one moved, they just stood there staring at the pavement. She got to her knees, but her head began to swim. As if he sensed what to do, Billy came to stand beside her, she put her arm around his neck and rested her head on his back. He stood there patiently waiting. When the dizziness had cleared, she managed to stand. 'Thank you for phoning for an ambulance,' she said, 'but you'll need to cancel it.' The group remained in a huddle. Not one person acknowledged her. What were they waiting for? Why were they standing around, staring at the spot where she'd been? She saw tears streaming down the van driver's face and placed a reassuring hand on his shoulder, 'Please don't be upset. Look at me, I'm fine. The accident was entirely my fault I know you weren't to blame.' He flicked a hand in her direction as though swatting a fly, but he didn't turn to look at her. She heard sirens in the distance and as the crowd turned towards the sound, she caught a glimpse of her body lying on the pavement beside Billy's. In that moment, she remembered. Now she understood what Myles had been trying to tell her. The golden light was hovering above Billy, she waited anxiously. He looked across at her body and then to where she was standing and without a backward glance he trotted over and sat to heel, eagerly looking up ready for his next command. 'Come on,' she said, stroking the dogs silky head, 'we're going home.'

Myles was exactly where she'd known he would be, sitting half way up the stairs. Billy let out a yelp and dashed over to greet him, excitedly weaving his body, in and out of his legs.

'Hello, old chap,' Myles laughed, ruffling the dog's ears.

With the greeting carried out to his satisfaction, Billy ran outside.

Lydia held back, lingering in the door way, just watching Myles. She hoped she didn't look too dishevelled, but she supposed getting run over was a pretty good excuse. It was certainly an improvement on the last time she had passed over. Being blown up by a German bomb had been somewhat startling.

'You're late,' he said, as she joined him on the stairs, 'they've started.'

'You should have given me a better clue,'

'Better clue! I thought I'd scuppered the whole damn show last night. You know perfectly well it's against the rules for those who've moved on to interfere.'

'You've done a pretty thorough job of interfering with me.'

He arched an eyebrow. 'Is that a complaint I hear?'

'Oh alright,' she sighed, snuggling against his shoulder, 'you've got me there. And I suppose even if I had remembered, I couldn't have done anything about it. Why did you try to make me remember anyway?'

'To make sure you'd know where to find me.'

'I see. So you thought I'd come back here just to find you, did you?' she teased 'No, I came back to see Pippa and Nick get married.'

He put his arm around her shoulders and pulled her into a kiss.

'Well, when you put it that way,' she sighed, 'How long do we have this time, before one of us is whisked away to a new existence?'

'Oh, about forever?' he whispered, his eyes twinkling.

'How do you mean forever?'

'Watch the ceremony,' he said, squeezing her hand.

'No, tell me now.'

'Oh alright. I didn't only come through to earth's parallel dimension because I wanted to help Polly and Frederick. I came because you needed me. It was you who brought me.'

'I did? How did I do that?'

'You made a wish,' he laughed, pulling her closer. 'Christ I was terrified waiting to come through. If I hadn't recognised your voice, I would have been stuck between dimensions. Not a place I'd care to revisit. When the planets started to shift, there seemed to be thousands of voices clamouring to be heard. I should have known I'd recognise yours straight away. We don't do very well apart, do we old girl?'

'Soul mates rarely do,' she agreed and kissed his cheek.

'Anyway, all things considered, it seems that after a century of trying, we've managed to put everything back on track in the celestial planes, and because of that, we can stay together.'

She looked down at Pippa and Nick, standing under the bridal arch, the epitome of a fairytale and so in love, that she doubted they'd even noticed she was missing.

Then she looked across to where Grant and Jenny were standing, they were holding hands. She nudged Myles.

'I know,' he said, following her gaze, 'they're going to be just fine those two.'

The service reached its natural conclusion and as Nick kissed his bride, everyone cheered. Almost everyone, Lydia noted, as Grant and Jenny sneaked a kiss of their own.

'Come on old girl,' Myles said, looking at his watch, 'time to go. Cartwright will be serving tea about now.'

They walked arm in arm up the stairs. Just before reaching the top, Lydia turned to blow a kiss down to the newlyweds. 'Have a happy life,' she whispered. Billy, hearing his whistle came scampering in from the garden and raced up the stairs after his mistress, scattering the dust motes dancing in the sunshine.

Acknowledgements

My grateful thanks to my husband Steve and son James for their support and particularly my youngest son Myles for the use of his name and his endless patience not only in reading my drafts but in helping me fathom the mysteries of IT.

To Lynn Varley for her encouragement and enthusiasm as my proof reader. Also, Howard and Elizabeth Briggs editor and publishers of my eBooks. They have supported me tirelessly in my quest to become a published author. Without their expertise, patience and encouragement, I would never have published a book at all.